Wic

MW00936879

Paranormal in Manhattan Mystery: Book 1

By LOTTA SMITH

Copyright

Prologue

966 Park Avenue Tower
11:48 AM, November 10…

With a weird moan, her whole body shivering, she collapses onto the sofa.

I think she's lucky that she's already sitting on the sofa as she crumples. If she was standing, she might have cracked her head on the marble floor like Humpty Dumpty—which won't be pretty.

She's lying there, totally motionless. One elbow's stiffly bent at a right angle, as if she's turned into stone as the result of looking Medusa in the eye.

I gasp—fearing she's dead.

Rick Rowling, the head of the FBI's New York Paranormal Division and my boss for the past two days, approaches and touches her neck. Looking totally blasé, he confirms that she's still alive.

I let out a sigh of relief.

On the other hand, Rowling announces that we leave the place because *"It's boring."*

My eyes widen with a total disbelief.

Of course, I disagree with him, but he brushes off my objection, stating that he doesn't care about all the crap of making arrests, prosecuting, and taking cases to trial. Again, he says that it's just a minor issue and he's way too busy for that. "You know what? I have better things to do," Rowling declares, turning on his heels to leave the condo.

"Excuse me, Rick," I call to his back.

"What?" he asks, without turning around.

"We can't just leave," I say. Then it suddenly occurs to me that offending my boss isn't in my best interest, so I add, "I'm afraid."

"Why not?" He cocks his head. "Mandy, don't be such a killjoy. The NYPD can work on the boring stuff, such as deciphering the social pathology of crimes and so on, because they have time to kill. On the other hand, I have no time to waste."

"Okay, so we don't need to decipher the social pathology of crimes, but we do need to figure out the whereabouts of the human-eating monster, don't we?" I point out.

I'm not joking or exaggerating.

I'm talking about a practically imperishable ghoul which could eat up the entire population of New York State, if not the whole world.

* * *

At precisely 2:13 in the morning, John Sangenis was standing in front of a shabby five-story apartment in Washington Heights. Fortunately, he didn't live there. He was just visiting Ivan Flynn, the insufferable asshole.

Usually, he had better things to do than visiting his worst enemy before the crack of dawn, such as sleeping like a log. Or making love with Ruth, which was even better than sleeping on his own. Ruth MacMahon was his girlfriend, who was unbelievably beautiful, dazzling, and had a truly big heart. Also, it didn't hurt that she was rich. What was more wonderful about her was she appreciated John's talent as an actor. It was a rare trait to come across in society, and it was why she happily provided him both moral and financial support.

If there were any shortcomings about her, it was that she was two-timing him with Ivan.

He thought about her taste in men, or lack thereof, and shrugged.

John wasn't the sharpest knife in the kitchen, so he didn't realize describing Ruth's taste in men as horrible was the same as admitting that he was a total loser.

A cold, wet late-autumn breeze was blowing from the East River. A sprinkle of rain hit him in the face. The metal stairs were slippery, occasionally letting out squeaks and squawks, as if the steel structure itself were threatening to fall into pieces any minute, which made John nervous. The building's elevator hadn't functioned since God knows when, so he had no choice but to climb up the damned stairs. Getting smashed with the lousy staircase like a piece of garbage wasn't high on his to-do list, so he ran up the stairs.

As an actor, he went to the gym to do occasional workouts and training, but that didn't mean he was a big fan of vigorous exercise. On normal days, he would have shied away from walking up the rusty metal stairs of a sad-looking apartment. Actually, he wouldn't have set a foot in this neighborhood unless he was starring in a gangster movie or TV show, hopefully as the lead role. After all, it wasn't the area where any of the characters of *Sex and the City* lived. It almost felt comical that this neighborhood was still included in Manhattan.

While he mentally dissed Washington Heights, he completely forgot about his own social status as one of the least important actors in off-Broadway theater scenes. He also conveniently forgot the fact that, if it weren't for the tiny apartment in Brooklyn, which he inherited from a late great-aunt, and financial assistance provided by Ruth, he couldn't even keep a roof over his head.

He jumped and let out a girly yelp when a rat the size of an obese Chihuahua ran up the stairs from behind and went ahead of him.

"What kind of miserable excuse of an unknown artist lives here?" he muttered to himself after some cussing—again, completely forgetting the fact he happened to be one of those miserable excuses himself.

As he approached the third floor where Ivan lived, John remembered his last exchange of words over the phone with his enemy, and being annoyed so greatly that he almost felt like his blood flowed backward.

About thirty minutes ago, he received a strange phone call from Ivan.

Getting a phone call from him was a rare event, mostly because the feeling of hate between the two of them was mutual. Both were Ruth's kept men, and both were trying their best to convince her that the other guy wasn't worth her time—or money.

"Hey, John the loser, I've got bad news for you," Ivan declared as soon as John picked up the call. He sounded like he was drunk, but there was something in his voice that made John nervous.

"What are you talking about?"

"I'm calling to deliver a piece of special news to you. Now that I've acquired something to make me the El Greco of the twenty-first century, you're so out of sight to Ruth and out of the picture. She is going to choose me, and she'll dump you like a piece of garbage. Ha! Why don't you curl up in the corner of your tiny apartment and cry like a little girl?" Then the line went dead.

Immediately, John rushed from his apartment and took a cab to Washington Heights. He was determined to confront the SOB and beat him till he cried like a baby.

As soon as he reached apartment 312, he banged on the door.

"Who's there?" Ivan's voice demanded from inside.

"It's John. Open up."

"No way."

"I have something to say to you. Open up!" John banged on the door even louder.

"Stop bothering me. Just leave!"

"No, I won't. I won't 'just leave' until I get to talk to you face-to-face."

"I have nothing to say to you. You have to leave, or else I'll call the cops and have you—"

It seemed Ivan was about to say "arrested," but his words stopped short.

Instead of menacing words, he let out an agonizing moan. It became louder and escalated to a high-pitched shriek.

Then came silence.

"Hey, Ivan, what's going on?" John asked as he switched from banging to knocking on the door.

No reply.

"Come on, Ivan. Open up. You can't fool me!" John yelled at the door, but again, no reply.

"Guess what, Ivan? You're all words and no action. You're just running away from me because I'm stronger than you. Ha!" John yelled at the door and turned on his heels to leave. After taking a couple of steps, he went back to his love opponent's door.

"Loser!" Yelling, he jumped and kicked at the door. He was just trying to make his point, but the worn-out door made of a thin veneer wood panel broke easily.

John lost his balance and fell onto the cold concrete corridor.

"Crap," he groaned.

Lying on the hard, cold floor, John was half expecting Ivan to come out of hiding, yelling at him, but no one came from inside. Instead, a twentyish Asian guy stormed out from next door.

"What is the matter with you?" he demanded.

John mumbled an apology and the guy went back to his room.

Something wasn't right.

He got up and reached for the now-broken door. It was locked, but he could put his hand inside to unlock the door.

Getting inside was a piece of cake.

"Hello?" John said. "Ivan? Um… Sorry about the door."

As he opened it, dim light came into his eyes. "Ivan…?"

There was no one in the room.

"What the hell…?" he muttered.

It was a tiny, one-bedroom, matchbox-sized apartment. In the living room / dining room / workroom was a 30" x 40" painting sitting on an easel. It was nothing fancy. The whole background was painted in an assortment of dark, boring, and depressing colors. The only part that caught his attention was the large blank area in the canvas. It looked as if whatever was portrayed had run out of the canvas and vanished.

He advanced closer to the painting.

On the side of the canvas, the title *G.H.O.U.L.* was written in pencil.

Glancing down, John gasped as he spotted an assortment of men's clothes, including underwear, heaped on the floor, as if someone stripped off those garments and left.

Or whoever had those garments on had disappeared like smoke.

"Hey, Ivan?" Not grasping the situation, John searched the apartment for his rival, but he couldn't find any signs of him.

John glared at the heap of clothes in front of the canvas for a while. Then, out of the blue, he kicked the garments. As the shirt, pants, and underwear scattered, something like pebbles of stone rolled over the floor.

"What the…?" John picked up a piece. It looked like a tooth—small, white, and hard, with a metal bolt on the base.

As an actor, he liked to play the role of a tough guy, but in reality, he wasn't. Startled, he dropped the tooth on the floor. When it hit, he caught a glimpse of several other pieces. Each was about the size of a chick pea, yellowish white with dark brown stains.

The moment he realized the stains might be blood, John passed out and dropped on the hard floor.

CHAPTER 1

Green and purple… Seriously? Who had the deciding vote in determining the color schemes of this hideous building? USCIS? Or FBI? I wondered as I stood in front of 26 Federal Plaza in Manhattan, my new workplace.

It was my first day of work at the FBI's New York Field Office, and I wasn't sure if I was happy or unhappy about my new career as an FBI special assistant.

If this were a book, movie, or TV show, I would be a budding FBI special agent or something really badass.

In that case, I would be ready to protect and defend the United States as I fought menacing terrorists or a group of evil aliens trying to invade Earth. In addition, if it were fiction, I would look like Jennifer Lawrence and have a really flashy educational background under my belt, such as having graduated from an Ivy League school at the top of my class. Not to mention I would be driving a Ferrari or a Lamborghini, or a Mercedes at least.

Unfortunately, none of the above characteristics applied. After all, I was talking about my life, and lately, it kind of sucked.

My name is Amanda Meyer. I'm a twenty-five-year-old American with Italian, English, and a little bit of Romanian heritage.

I'm an American woman in my mid-twenties, but that's all I have in common with *The Hunger*

Games star. I stand at 5'4", and I'm a size or two—or maybe three—larger than her dress size.

I don't have an Ivy League education under my belt, mostly because Harvard, Yale, Columbia, and all other such schools rejected my application. As for the car, I don't even own one. I used to drive a relatively new Toyota Camry, but I sold it. I was trying my best to convince myself I didn't need to have a car anymore now that I moved back to my parents' home in Queens, New York.

About a month ago, I was a medical student in North Carolina. I was in my third year—busy studying for exams, memorizing all the medical and surgical knowledge, and doing clinical rotations—until I got kicked out of medical school.

Don't get me wrong. I wasn't a bad student.

So I didn't hold high hopes of graduating at the top of my class, or someday becoming a Nobel laureate. Then again, my academic performance wasn't that bad. I was usually at around the top 50-60 percent of the class. At a place where the majority of your classmates have an IQ of 180 and up, even being a mediocre student took lots and lots of hard work.

Anyway, the odds of my finishing medical school and becoming a doctor or getting some cushy job with some pharma/biotech/insurance company were pretty high. Back then, I used to picture myself in the future driving a nice car and vacationing in beautiful resorts.

Generally speaking, doctors are highly regarded in today's society. Sometimes, people talked about the top-notch physicians in comparison with God. On the other hand, I was held in comparison with the Grim Reaper and the Angel of Death. And as a result, I got kicked out of medical school, saying good-bye to my life plan as a doctor.

Oh, did I mention getting kicked out of medical school didn't offset my larger-than-life student loan?

So, there I stood, with no degree under my belt and a huge debt up to my eyeballs. To rub salt in the wound, Justin, my now ex-fiancé, had called off our engagement. We went to the same med school. He was two years my senior and was already in his first year of residency training. Obviously, he had assessed the pros and cons of staying with me and concluded that staying with a woman called the Grim Reaper wasn't likely to boost his value as a surgeon.

As I stood in front of the East German-style building, I felt so depressed, I almost started sobbing.

Look at the bright side, Mandy... I tried to convince myself.

At least I was going to have a job, and their offer wasn't bad. I would be able to make monthly payments on my student loan and make a decent living. Maybe I could even move out of my parents' townhouse in a year or so.

Actually, I wasn't eager to take this job when I received the offer, but Mom and Dad insisted I should. They were not very keen on spending the rest of their lives paying off my student loan.

"Miss, you've been standing here for a long time." Frowning, the guy in a guard's uniform gave me an accusing glare.

"Um... I'm sorry. I got a little bit distracted. I'm supposed to start working here today," I said, but based on his deep frown, I was positive he didn't believe me.

"Oh, I'm running late. I've got to go...." I attempted to walk away, but he grabbed my arm.

"What is the purpose of—?" the guard started interrogating me, but he didn't get to finish his sentence.

"Good morning, Stanley," a male voice boomed from behind us. It was a deep, smooth baritone—clear, calm, and confident. Without turning back to see him, I found myself picturing a tall guy with a certain level of sexiness. He continued, "For your information, you don't want to mess with her. Guess what? So far, she's killed three men just by touching them. In addition, it's her first day working as my assistant. If you convince her to leave without even starting the job, Hernandez will be so pissed."

I had a remote knowledge that the head of the FBI's New York Office was named Hernandez.

"Mr. Rowling!" The guard's response sounded more like a surprise than an acknowledgement.

When he straightened himself, he was no longer grabbing my arm, too busy saluting Mr. Rowling.

"I am awfully sorry for my rude behavior. I didn't know she was your new assistant."

Then, turning to me, he apologized profusely. "I'm awfully sorry, ma'am."

If eyes could speak, his were saying, 'Why didn't you mention you worked for *him*?'

"Okay, so we're all cool," said Mr. Rowling.

I turned back to thank and greet him, but words failed me.

He was tall, athletic, and had broad shoulders. He had flawless fair skin and dark hair styled in a conservatively messy 'do. His mesmerizing green eyes looked almost blue, and his cheekbones were prominent. His nose and jaw were sculpted to perfection.

In a nutshell, he was drop-dead gorgeous.

But that wasn't the only reason I was at a loss for words.

"You are the—" Clenching my teeth and fists, I searched for words.

Though I didn't remember his name, I did recognize him, in an 'I am so going to kill him if I ever lay my eyes on him again' way.

"Yeah, I'm Rick Rowling." He flashed his perfect set of pearly whites. Obviously, he didn't read my mind. "Hi, Mandy. Nice meeting you again." He extended his right hand toward me.

I took a deep breath. I had no fucking idea why this guy was so familiar with me to call me by the nickname I'd used since kindergarten. Before today, we had met only once for just a couple of hours, and during that short period of time, he killed my future as a doctor.

I took his hand, half wishing he'd drop dead on the spot.

After all, he was the one who convinced the Chapel Hill Police Department and my medical school that I'm the Grim Reaper.

CHAPTER 2

"You're very welcome," Rowling said while walking me into the building.

"Excuse me?" was my reply. I didn't thank him, and I had no intention of doing so.

"Hasn't your mom told you to say thank you when someone helps you?" He arched an eyebrow. "If I recall it right, it's not the first time I've saved your behind. Oh, don't say you don't remember how I got you out of jail. Otherwise, you would still be in the middle of a triple-murder trial."

"Hello? That wasn't going to happen, as I didn't kill anyone," I retorted, following him into the elevator. "That was a false accusation."

"Ha! Haven't you ever heard about the tales of innocent citizens serving twenty-plus years in prison for a crime they didn't commit?" Rowling snorted as he punched the Door Close button.

"Okay, thank you so much for facilitating the process of proving my innocence for the alleged triple murder," I said through clenched teeth. "Then again, you didn't need to give them the impression I'm the Grim Reaper!"

"Don't be upset. I didn't tell them you're the Grim Reaper. I just advised them not to touch you unless they have suicidal wishes," he said matter-of-factly. "It's true those guys, who slipped out of the judiciary system without getting the penalties they deserved, died just minutes after you touched them. You should be proud of yourself. After all, you made the world a better place by killing them."

"I didn't kill them!" I snapped.

"Whatever." He shrugged.

"You know what? I got kicked out of medical school because of your stupid remark to the police force in Chapel Hill."

"That means you don't have to spend the rest of your life surrounded by germs, sick people, and misery. Lucky you." He smiled like an angel.

"That's not my point!" I shrieked, partly because he was sort of right. It was true I often fantasized about winning a jackpot with Powerball, paying off my student loan, and leaving medicine for good. Then again, quitting on my own was one thing, while being forced to leave was a totally different story.

"Besides that, what I mentioned was nothing but my personal opinion. It's not my fault they chose to believe it. They could have laughed it off as a stupid joke, which they didn't."

He had a point. I sighed.

As the elevator door opened, he held it for me, and this time, I thanked him. It was true that I was upset about him, but I had to show I had manners.

It's true I have manners, but it's also true that I tend to lose balance at the wrong place at the worst possible time. When I walked out of the elevator, I tripped over nothing. For a moment, I felt like I was flying, but at the same time, I was aware of gravity kicking in. While I was falling, many thoughts crossed my mind. *Is it possible to crack my head like Humpty Dumpty in the federal building's elevator and die? If I get injured, disabled, or die, will I be able to pay off my student loan with the settlement? Yeah, perhaps falling might not be that bad....*

And the next thing, I was in his arms. No. Technically, I was in his arm because he was holding me tightly against his chest only using one arm. Without thinking, I inhaled his clean, wholesome, and… alluring scent. He smelled of fresh linen, citrus, and deep blue ocean—Mediterranean Sea, perhaps. It was addictive. I inhaled deeply.

"Are you okay?" he whispered.

I looked up at his face and lost my words. I knew he was good-looking, but with a close-up view of his beautifully sculpted face and the captivating green eyes, I realized how hot he was. As I witnessed the green of his eyes deepen, I half expected him to clasp me tighter and start stroking my face with his other hand—or, even better, kiss me—totally like *Fifty Shades of Grey.*

But that didn't happen.

Instead of caressing my face with a sensual touch of his long fingers, he patted my cheek with the other hand like a jerk. "You don't need to fake a stumble in order to cling to me. All you have to do is ask, or just hug me as much as you want to."

"I didn't fake a stumble!" Pulling myself out of his embrace, I retorted, "I happen to be a tad bit on the clumsy side. Don't flatter yourself."

"Now you're playing hard to get, huh?" He was grinning from ear to ear. "By the way, Hernandez wants to see you."

"Hernandez who? As in, the head of the FBI in the New York Field Office?" I asked, puzzled. I couldn't understand why he'd bother to meet someone as insignificant as a newbie assistant.

"Yes." Rowling nodded. "Go upstairs and turn left. The corner office is the one Hernandez occupies. My office is in the right corner. Meet me as soon as you're finished with the old guy."

* * *

It started with three sudden deaths of my patients.

I was in the middle of clinical rotations and the patients dropped dead when I touched them.

Yeah, you heard me right. I touched the patients I was supposed to look after and they dropped dead. To be precise, three patients died just minutes after I touched them in three consecutive days.

The first patient was Mr. Jack T. Simmons, who was visiting the outpatient clinic complaining of a sore throat. He had a massive heart attack as soon as I touched his hand to take his pulse. The next day, I was running a preliminary physical exam on Mr. Patrick Barnes, who had a minor stomachache. When I tried to listen to his heart using the stethoscope, I touched his chest. He had a massive brain hemorrhage and died on the spot. Neither of them had a preexisting condition that could have caused them to die so suddenly.

And on the third day, I was helping Mr. Caleb Schumacher, who was visiting the outpatient clinic because of a twisted ankle. I palpated his leg to see the maximum point of tenderness, and he broke out into hives. He then started wheezing and clutching his chest. Before I had time to say "Emergency!" he was a dead man. The cause of his death was anaphylactic shock, a massive allergic reaction, but what caused it was never identified.

People die for many reasons, but having three patients with no preexisting life-threatening conditions dropping dead while they were under my care in three consecutive days didn't spotlight my performance in a good way. Actually, everyone cast me suspicious looks. As a result, I was detained by the Chapel Hill Police Department as a serial murder suspect.

The police had conducted a thorough investigation of me. They went so far as to analyze all the garments, including bras and panties, I wore at the time of the incidents. I'm not a slob, so I had washed and dried the clothes I had on during the first episodes, and the police accused me of tampering with evidence. I told them I never skipped laundry because I couldn't stand the idea of having my dirty clothes staying dirty overnight, facilitating the growth and proliferation of potentially harmful microorganisms.

"Oh, yeah?" one of the detectives said sarcastically. "You can't stand having dirty clothes around you."

"You can't stand having dirty men around you, can you?" another detective chimed in.

"What do you mean?"

"Guess what? In the past, all three of the men were arrested for killing and/or raping little girls; however, they were released because of holes in the case, such as an accidental destruction of DNA in the lab. They walked as free men. You couldn't tolerate seeing them go unpunished, and that's why you killed them. Right?"

"I didn't kill them!"

The conversation between the detectives and yours truly didn't go very smoothly.

There was no physical evidence to charge me for three first-degree murders, mostly because I killed no one; however, the lack of physical evidence made it even more difficult to prove my innocence.

When the investigation hit a dead end, this gorgeous guy appeared in the uncomfortable interrogation room of the Chapel Hill Police Department. Without even introducing himself, he started asking me questions. To my surprise, the detectives didn't object to having a total stranger interrogating me.

After a couple of hours, he said something that sounded almost like a sick joke.

"First of all, she didn't kill those men—at least not intentionally. It's just she happens to be something like, say, the Grim Reaper. That's why those criminals dropped dead the moment she touched them."

I expected the detectives to get really annoyed by his stupid remark, or crack up laughing like jerks, but they didn't. Soon, the chief of the Chapel Hill Police Department himself came into the room where I was being held. Apologizing profusely, he released me, admitting it was atrociously wrong to detain me.

The detectives and police officers avoided having any physical contact with me, as if they believed the handsome man's silly words. He was already gone when I was released. I wished I could say "Thank you" to him.

I went back to the normalcy of my life. Or, at least, I thought so.

At that time, I was going to return to school and continue my education, but they didn't welcome me back with open arms.

They were all about this stupid rumor that I was the Grim Reaper, or the Angel of Death, and also started avoiding physical contact with me at all costs. When my fiancé broke up with me, he communicated with me by text message.

The board of directors ran a quick assessment of the pros and cons of keeping me registered as a student, and they came to a conclusion to dismiss me pronto. Obviously, they didn't think having someone nicknamed the Grim Reaper was a very good idea.

It was like I had suddenly contracted some deadly and incurable infectious disease, such as Ebola.

According to the social understandings, medical professionals are supposed to be super-logical and scientific; however, people in this community also happen to be big on superstition. Maybe dealing with life and death had that effect on them. Oh, did I mention rumors spread faster than the speed of light in the medical community?

I wasn't a rocket scientist, but putting two and two together was an easy task. I knew it was him. Though the chief of police never admitted it, I knew it was the guy who butted into my interrogation who spread the word that I was the Grim Reaper.

CHAPTER 3

After I finished meeting with Assistant Director in Charge Sheldon Hernandez, my brain was smoking with confusion.

Unlike what I had anticipated, the head of the FBI's New York Office treated me like a very important guest. Though maybe "sacrifice" was a more appropriate word than "guest."

"Did you have a chance to touch Rowling?" were Hernandez's first words.

"Yes," I answered, and he clicked his tongue.

"Assuming we're not in need of an ambulance, he didn't die on the spot, did he?" Hernandez was a broad-shouldered, heavyset man in his mid-forties sporting bushy eyebrows. While he spoke, his bushy eyebrows were furrowed as if they were holding their own breath.

I didn't know the right response, so I just shook my head. "No."

"Damn." Then he mumbled, "Then again, considering USCAB is a huge post-retirement job provider for us, having the only son of the CEO killed might not be such a great idea."

"USCAB? Isn't that a security company?" I asked. If I recalled correctly, USCAB—United States Cover All Bases—was a conglomerate of security, insurance, real estate, and several more fields.

Hernandez cleared his throat. "I thought you knew about your direct superior's background."

"No, I don't."

"Good. That explains why you took this job offer." He smiled.

I felt trapped. My gut instinct was screaming, "You shouldn't have taken this job!" At the same time, the little white angel on my shoulder was whispering, "Then again, considering all the other potential employers rejected your application, you need to keep this job. You know it's next to impossible to pay off your debt, which is larger than a quarter million dollars, working at Walmart or Starbucks."

Looking at my sullen face, he continued. "Ms. Meyer, you should be proud of yourself. It's the first time Rowling has asked for someone specific to work as his subordinate. Anyway, I believe you two will get along well."

"Sir, why was I hired?" I asked. "Not that I'm complaining, but I have no suitable background for the FBI."

"That's a good question." He smiled, which meant he was contemplating a plausible answer. He cleared his throat. "We reviewed your qualifications when Rowling requested you to be his assistant. So, you went to medical school, and you were in the middle of clinical rotations, am I correct?"

"Yes."

"I believe you have encountered difficult patients, and maybe a moody attending physician or two."

"Yes, I have." I nodded. "Many of those types of people."

"Excellent. That makes you a great assistant. At times, Rowling can be quite difficult. I had been looking for someone who can steer him in the right direction—especially when collaborating with different branches of law enforcement. Perhaps you've heard or read before, but the relationship between the NYPD and us is best described as complex. Making it lousier isn't in our best interest. Think of him like one of those difficult patients and temperamental physicians all rolled into one, and throw in a spoiled five-year-old. Oh, and don't forget he's a genius when it comes to offending the people the bureau doesn't want to offend. You get the picture, right?"

"I think so." I resisted the urge to roll my eyes.

"He tends to create unneeded tension and trouble, especially in the wrong place and at the wrong time. Perhaps he's doing it on purpose…." As he spoke, his hands clenched into fists, and his knuckles whitened. "Anyway, I hope you'll manage to steer him clear of trouble."

"I can try," I said.

He wished me luck on my new career, and the meeting was over.

"By the way, Ms. Meyer," he said to my back, "I believe you're used to witnessing strange things."

"Yes, I suppose so." After all, having three people dying minutes after touching me qualified as strange events.

"Very good. Excellent," he said.

When I left his office, I was welcomed by a crowd of applauding special agents and special assistants. They praised my selfless decision to take this job. Some of them were even teary. Then again, none of them tried to shake hands with me.

Obviously, they were happy to have me as Rick Rowling's assistant. At first, I didn't know why, but then I caught a couple men cheering and high-fiving, and overheard, "Thank God he got an assistant before he laid his eyes on us! We're safe. Yeah!" At that point, I knew why they were so ecstatic about me joining the FBI—none of them wanted to work with him.

I felt terrible for taking the offered salary without negotiation. I shouldn't have believed what the recruiter said. He told me it was a challenging, exciting, yet very stable job with nice pay, and I believed him.

When I finally reached the office of my new boss, I froze in shock.

The door was ordinary, but the metal panel on the door read Paranormal Cases Division.

At first, I thought it might be a typo, but I didn't know any words that could be misspelled as "paranormal." If I recalled right, I was never informed about coping with supernatural beings, such as vampires, werewolves, and ghosts.

"Mr. Rowling, is the panel on the door a joke?" I confronted my new boss, who was sitting at a huge mahogany desk. I had seen a similar one at a former professor's house. He was a WASP—White, Anglo-Saxon, Protestant—coming from old money. He loved having parties so he could show off his glamorous life and super-fabulous estate to his students. The desk was an antique from the eighteenth century.

"What's the big deal?" He arched an eyebrow. "Paranormal Cases Division is the official name of this division."

"Such a division isn't listed on the FBI website," I pointed out. "You know paranormal is about ghosts, aliens, and UFOs, right? Do I look like an idiot who believes such an outrageous section actually exists?"

"You know what? There are many kinds of sections and departments dealing with such lives, and our particular division happens to be one of them."

"Mr. Rowling, you're joking, aren't you?"

"Oh, don't forget we also deal with vampires. By the way, drop the 'Mr.' and call me Rick, okay?"

"Okay," I said, and added, "Rick."

"Good. Have you ever seen *Ghostbusters*? Hey, stop rolling your eyes. According to that movie, the Big Apple happens to be America's most haunted city, which is probably true. Perhaps you've heard of a scandalous tale or two involving non-human existences such as ghosts, spirits, aliens and the like. And guess what? Someone has to deal with them to keep the power balance in this town."

"All right. Assuming that paranormal lives actually exist, why doesn't the government tell the general public about our supernatural neighbors?"

"Like 'Breaking News: Your neighbors might be Martians, and your doctor might be a zombie!'? Don't be ridiculous. Besides, those who are acquainted with paranormal presences are already aware of them, and the rest of the world need not know or learn about them. Informing the entire city sounds as good a plan as pushing the panic button."

"Okay, I get your point."

"Good. Any more questions?" he asked, shifting on the chair and crossing his long legs.

"Yes. What made you hire me as your subordinate?"

"That's simple." He shrugged. "First of all, I need an assistant who takes care of my daily chores, such as making case files. Writing case files is almost like writing your patients' charts, so I believe that part will be easy for you. I've had my share of assistants, but for some unknown reasons, they quit within a month or so. Those losers. Can you believe one of them quit on the second day? In addition, the people I deal with are not necessarily ladies and gentlemen, so having someone with a reputation as the Grim Reaper helps."

"Excuse me?" I narrowed my eyes. "How many times do I have to remind you that I'm not the Grim Reaper?"

"That's what you say." He winked.

I clenched my fists. I was tempted to whack him in his beautiful face and storm out of the room for good. The only reason I didn't was my humongous student loan; like it or not, I could at least stay up to date with the payment as long as I kept this job.

In addition, this job was starting to look something like an au pair for a psychiatric patient. Indeed, Rick Rowling reminded me of the people in mental facilities. I had seen more than my share of patients with conditions such as grandiose/persecutory delusional disorders. Also, other than mental patients, Rick Rowling was the only person who talked about supernatural lives so breezily, like discussing the weather.

Yeah, right.

I had a lightbulb moment.

As I recalled Hernandez's advice to see Rowling as the combination of a difficult patient and a temperamental attending physician, I realized this guy was mentally ill. Perhaps the part about him being the only son of USCAB's CEO was true. I could imagine filthy rich people with tons of money had the power to persuade a government office into hiring their son. I recalled how Rick Castle of *Castle* got into the NYPD by utilizing his friendship with the mayor of New York City so he could tag along with that beautiful female detective. In addition, Rowling was the only guy in this office wearing a Versace suit.

"Okay. Now I understand." I smiled.

Albeit limited, I had experience dealing with mentally ill patients. I knew for a fact that any endeavor, such as trying to decipher the patients' stories of menacing aliens snooping on their thoughts, never worked.

Okay, so my latest theory of Rick Rowling being a nutjob impersonating an FBI agent had some holes, such as, it didn't explain why his words were convincing enough to label me as the Grim Reaper. Then again, a desperate time called for a desperate measure. I was more than happy to believe what *I* wanted to believe.

My smile widened. All I needed to do was pretend to listen to his story. Maybe my new career path wasn't that bad. I had compared my pay to that of a first-year resident's, and mine was slightly better. Considering I didn't need to look after drug addicts and HIV-positive people, this could be a cushy job.

"Nice to meet you, Rick. We'll work together as a team, you know," I declared.

"That's what I've been trying to tell you for the past hour." He shrugged.

There was a knock on the door, so I began my duties and answered it. It was another special assistant with two women. Both of them were stunningly beautiful. One was in her late twenties to early thirties. From her looks and fashion, she reminded me of a cast member from *The Real Housewives of New York City*. The other woman was a few years younger than her, probably in her mid-twenties. They had resemblances in the shapes of the nose and jaw, so I presumed them to be sisters.

The younger of the two looked more delicate than the other; if the elder sister was a sunflower, she was baby's breath.

"Agent Rowling, you have visitors asking for your services," the assistant said.

CHAPTER 4

Rowling asked me to step out of the office so he could speak with the 'visitors' in private.

"Hey, I didn't know you guys set up occasional visitors as well," I said to the guy who brought in the women as soon as we stepped into the hallway. "You know, I thought of the FBI as a serious government office, but now it's starting to feel as if I'm working at a movie studio, like Universal Studios Hollywood."

"Excuse me?" He frowned as if he didn't get what I was talking about.

"I know what this is all about." I winked conspiratorially. "This is just a silly role-play for this Rick Rowling guy, right? He's a head case who believes he's an FBI agent when, actually, he happens to be a mental patient who needs serious institutionalization. So, I'm guessing the parts about his dad being filthy rich and providing many jobs for retired personnel of this agency are true. Anyway, you're all pretending he's an FBI agent and not a nutjob with a grandiose delusional disorder with a little touch of a personality disorder, right?"

"No!" His eyes widened in what seemed like horror.

Smack!

I felt a sharp pain on the back of my head.

"Ouch!" I looked back and met eye-to-eye with Rowling, who'd just smacked my head with a rolled *Wall Street Journal*.

"I heard that!" He snapped, arms crossed.

"Police brutality!" I protested.

"I'm a special agent in charge, not a police officer." Rowling stuck out his tongue like a brat. Uncrossing his arms, he continued. "It looks like you're much denser than I expected. Killing your medical career before you had a chance to make horrible misdiagnoses might be the best thing I've done for society."

"Hello? I could have become a great doctor." Rubbing the back of my head, I protested, "I could have helped millions of sick people."

Responding to my protest with a snort, Rowling turned to the special assistant. "Tennyson, I need three coffees: one black and two decafs. In addition, tell the queen of denial here more about her job description, so she understands the Paranormal Cases Division does exist in the FBI's New York Field Office. Also, it's safe to touch her so long as you're not a killer or a rapist who previously slipped through the cracks. If she keeps operating in a denial mode, you can just hit or kick her."

"Yes, sir!" Tennyson said.

"Come on, you can't just abuse me like I'm some sort of criminal," I protested, but Tennyson rushed me to the kitchenette and gave me a huge lecture about my job.

When I was summoned back to Rowling's office thirty minutes later, I was slightly smarter than before. Okay, so it wasn't like my IQ level had significantly improved in such a short time, but at least I understood there was no way out of this job.

To my astonishment, the Paranormal Cases Division did exist.

After serving coffee to my new boss and his visitors, Tennyson took me to the Special Evidence room and showed me case files. One of them contained the photographs of what looked like mummified corpses. They didn't come from ancient Egypt, the Mayans, or the Aztecs, but the modern-day Bronx. According to him, they were the victims of a vampire, who went on a killing spree until Rowling took the matter into his hands. In the refrigerator, there was a hand of an extraterrestrial. It looked almost identical to the one in the *Predator* room at Planet Hollywood in Las Vegas. I commented as such, and he responded with, "Yeah, that's what I thought at first, but believe me, the one at Planet Hollywood doesn't move."

A superior woman would have conducted a close examination of the hand, and a lesser woman would have fainted like a lady from the nineteenth century. I was only myself, so I backed up when I caught a slight movement of the hand in a tamper-proof container.

In addition, Tennyson walked me through Rowling's credentials, including but not limited to his educational background at MIT as a physics major and at the University of Maryland graduate school as a criminology and criminal justice major. Tennyson didn't forget to mention the part that Rowling graduated from both schools at the top of his class.

He also told me truly paranormal and metaphysical events tended to happen whenever my boss was involved. According to him, Rowling practically had every scandal and weakness of the top executives of the FBI, CIA, and even local police forces at his fingertips. Obtaining this kind of information was a piece of cake for him, by utilizing his own information network and that of USCAB's. So basically, he always got whatever he wanted. Even the director of the FBI in DC had no power over him. To make things even worse, Rowling's case closure rate was slightly higher than 100 percent.

"The case closure rate cannot surpass 100 percent," I pointed out. "That's mathematically impossible."

"Yes, it can." He shrugged. "He often sniffs out cases and closes them, typically wreaking havoc, which makes the rate higher."

"Oh…." I rolled my eyes. "Sounds like a troublemaker."

"A trouble-generator is probably more accurate. He absolutely loves trouble."

"How does he sniff out cases before they become cases? Does he have this little bird who whispers about new ones in his ears?"

When I said that, I was feeling a little bit sarcastic, but he didn't seem to take it.

"Well, that's close, if not very accurate," he said. "Actually, he has this gift. He knows if a person is dead or alive just by looking at a photograph of them."

I opened my mouth like a moron.

"You don't need to believe me." He shrugged. "If I were in your position, I wouldn't believe such a ridiculous story."

"Okay, I can't say if I believe you or not, but I'll try to remember your words." I nodded.

"Good. Zombie Repellant is what we call him," Tennyson told me, to wrap things up.

"Zombie Repellant?" I parroted.

"Yeah, meaning that even zombies won't go near him."

"Were there any zombie cases in the past?"

"No. Not yet." He chuckled. "It's just a figure of speech. By the way, I guess I know why he made a special request to hire you as his assistant. You're funny, Mandy."

I didn't know whether to be flattered or offended. I had never felt more uncertain about my future. For once, I thought getting kicked out of medical school might not be that bad, but I wasn't keen on encountering paranormal beings. I found myself wondering which would be worse—dealing with drug addicts and sick people or possibly dealing with blood-sucking monsters.

When I went back to my superior's office, the visitors had already left.

"We've got an assignment, and I bet your firstborn you'll see something sensational," he announced, holding a photograph of a young Caucasian guy sporting a cocky grin.

"Please do not bet my firstborn who's not even born."

Rowling clicked his tongue. "You have no sense of humor."

"I didn't know I was summoned just to be insulted."

"Anyway, an acquaintance of my acquaintance's acquaintance was involved in an incident," he said, completely ignoring my words of resistance.

According to him, the two beautiful female visitors were Beth and Ruth MacMahon. Beth, the elder of the duo, was the one he knew. It was about her younger sister Ruth's boyfriend, who disappeared in a strange circumstance.

"So, what's your relationship with Beth?" I

asked casually, expecting an answer in line of something like a neighbor.

"She's my old man's lover," he stated matter-of-factly.

"Old man? You mean, like your father?"

"I don't call my mother an old man."

I recalled Tennyson's lecture. Daniel Rowling, my boss's father, was a former director of the FBI. After his retirement, he became the CEO of USCAB, taking over from his father who had founded the company, and expanded the business to a Fortune 500 company. According to Tennyson, Daniel Rowling was a real billionaire who was about to join the trillionaires' club.

"Speaking of mother, what's your mom's take on his having a lover outside their marriage?" I asked, curiosity getting the better of my manners.

"Which one?" Rowling cocked his head to the side.

"Well, most people have just one mom."

"I'm not most people," he pointed out. "The biological one went out of my life when I was three. She's happily divorced and pursuing her new and old career as an artist in Melbourne with a beau younger than me. Considering she never remarried, she isn't stupid, I guess. As for the other woman I used to call 'Mother,' she died ten years ago, complications from multiple sclerosis."

"I'm sorry."

"For what?"

"I'm sorry for your loss, and for asking a nosy question."

"Never mind." He shrugged. "I didn't know Beth was still in the city. Considering the old fart is on a business trip in Tokyo for two more weeks, he's going to find women there."

That was too much information. I didn't know what to say, so I kept my mouth shut.

"Anyway, Beth is Miss Tuesday," he said abruptly.

"Miss Tuesday?" I parroted.

"Yup. The old bastard has five girlfriends. Each woman is in charge of a specific day of the week from Monday to Friday. He calls Saturday and Sunday 'freedom days' and does highly unethical activities. Talk about the enemy of moral standards."

I rolled my eyes. "Sounds like a tough guy. How old is he?"

"He should be seventy, unless he's cheating social security."

Having five lovers at the age of seventy? That was outstanding, yet bordering on gross.

"So, what about Ruth? Is she Miss Monday?"

"Wrong. She's Miss Wednesday."

"What…?" My jaw dropped to the floor.

"I was kidding. Ruth has a boyfriend. Actually, she has not one but two boyfriends. Well, the number is not the issue, as she can have as many boyfriends as she likes. One of them is a vain painter, the other a vain actor infesting off-Broadway. Both of them blame the ignorant society that doesn't appreciate their *great* genius for the lack of their success."

"Sounds familiar."

"Yeah, right. The kind of pathetic excuse of artists whose best expertise is beautifying the fact that they can't make ends meet," he spat. "Anyway, some women fall for their type, and Ruth happens to be one of them. She has a good education and she's not particularly ugly, but the rest is history. She's been with not just one but two pathetic losers, happily providing them with moral and financial support. What's her problem?"

"There's no accounting for taste," I commented.

"As a consequence of having bad taste in men, one of her boyfriends has gone missing, and the other is being held as a murder suspect at the 34th Precinct of the NYPD. Let's go see the loser."

"Which one of the boyfriends is missing?"

"The painter," he answered. Staring at the photograph, he continued. "He's dead." His tone was unemotional, as if he were talking about weather.

I was still skeptical about Tennyson's words regarding Rowling's gift to see if a person was dead or alive just by looking at photographs. "How do you know if he's dead when his body hasn't been recovered?"

"Mandy, how do you kill douche bags just by touching them?" he countered.

"I didn't kill them!"

"Then again, they dropped dead, and no one can provide a plausible explanation to the incidents. Shit happens." He shrugged, and then he explained the case. A man called Ivan Flynn disappeared, and the way it happened was far from normal. He vanished, leaving his garments and shoes remaining in a heap.

Ivan Flynn graduated from a top art college more than ten years ago, and he was still waiting to be discovered. He'd recently switched his career path from fine art to commercial illustrator. Apparently, he believed illustration wasn't *real* art, but the job was easier and the pay was better—which was the reason for the change in Flynn's career path, provided by

Ruth. I'm not an illustrator, but the moment I heard about this, I hated Ivan.

He'd landed a gig for an online gaming program featuring wizards, warriors, and monsters. Actually, it was Ruth who set up the deal, but she opted not to tell Ivan for the fear of damaging his pride.

"Damaging his pride? Talk about exaggeration!" Rowling laughed his as... I mean, *behind* off when mentioning this part.

Ivan started working on the project, isolating himself in a shabby apartment he called the "atelier."

Meanwhile, John Sangenis, a stage actor and Ruth's other boyfriend, was as unsuccessful as Ivan in his field. They loathed each other like Lindsay Lohan and Amanda Bynes, only cattier and less famous, which made sense because losing Ruth meant losing the bread from the mouths of both boys.

Late in the night, John paid a visit to Ivan's tiny apartment. According to John, Ivan had called him and declared his victory in the war of conquering Ruth's heart. John didn't take it very well and went straight to Ivan's atelier, determined to punch him.

Ivan answered John's knock without opening the door. After a noisy verbal altercation, John ended up smashing through the cheap door by kicking it. When he came inside, Ivan, who was arguing with him only a minute before, was nowhere to be seen.

Responding to a neighbor's noise complaint, a police officer arrived to find John lying on the floor passed out and a huge candle burning.

At first, this incident was considered to be a late-night fight and vandalism until the police found a dental implant and bone fragments scattered around an unconscious John Sangenis. Forensic analysis confirmed the bone fragments as parts of Ivan Flynn's pelvis. And after confirming the implant's owner as Ivan from the serial number, the dentist told the police that her patient came to her office earlier on the day of his disappearance; when she saw him, the implant was securely attached to his jawbone.

John Sangenis became the prime suspect of a murder case.

CHAPTER 5

We drove to the NYPD's 34th Precinct in a metallic silver Ferrari, Rick Rowling's personal car.

Yeah, you heard me right—I was riding in *the* Ferrari.

I had seen the pricy Italian vehicle numerous times, mostly in the parking lot of the medical school I used to attend, but it was my first time actually riding in it. And I had to admit, I more than perked up when I saw the car.

"I'm the assistant. I'll drive!" I volunteered.

"In your dreams, pal." Rowling dismissed my offer and slipped into the driver's seat.

I tried my best to convince him the importance of letting his assistant chauffeur him around, but he didn't even let me touch the key. How ungenerous of him.

Riding with him was a hellish experience—he drove as if he were in the Daytona 500, not the middle of Manhattan.

"Are you insane?" I managed to say while I tried my best not to puke in the passenger's seat. "Seriously, you should give your driver's license back to the state. You can't drive like a meth-crazed maniac!"

"Ha. They shouldn't grant a driver's license to someone incapable of dodging my car" was his reply.

He had a point, so I made a mental note to file a complaint to the local DMV.

"So, what are you going to do at the station?"

I asked. If his investigative style was as outrageous as his driving, trouble was bound to happen. In addition, if I recalled it right, NYPD and the FBI were different organizations.

"I'll ask questions and, if applicable, I'll arrest the criminal," he said in a singsong voice.

"Remember, the NYPD is in charge of this case, and don't forget you can't arrest someone without a warrant," I warned him between retching. *I should have taken a Dramamine before taking this ride from Hell.*

"Mandy, since when did you become an expert to tell me how to do my job?"

"Since I was briefed on your inclination for causing trouble and offending people the bureau doesn't want to offend. I heard about how you ticked off the detectives at the 34th Precinct by interfering with their investigation *and* stealing the credit for the case."

"Ha. I didn't *steal* the credit. It was so mine." He snorted. "We need a warrant to arrest someone. Then again, we don't need a warrant to kill."

"You can't kill people, with or without a warrant!" I spat. Then I added, "Rick, can you please behave like a responsible adult at the NYPD?" Okay, considering the length of our relationship had been just a couple hours, I was no expert on Rick Rowling. Then again, I recognized trouble when I saw it. And I was 100 percent sure that Rick Rowling was big trouble.

"Hey, Mandy, will you stop lecturing me like you're talking to a three-year-old?" Rowling made tsk-tsk sounds.

"By the way, how did Beth MacMahon meet your dad?" I asked, in an attempt to distract him.

"She was hired to do flower arrangements at some reception for USCAB. Beth is quite successful and well-known in the world of floral arrangement. She's been seeing him for a couple of years, I believe."

I wondered why he knew so much about his father's love life, but I was too modest to further inquire on that subject.

"My old man's into women with their own skills and expertise," he continued. "He keeps his distance from trophy-mistress types. Women who can make their own successful businesses are his forte."

"Wow, sounds like friends with awesome benefits. Perhaps those businesses have dual missions as intel bases," I muttered.

"Yeah, right. Why do you think that?"

"It was supposed to be a joke."

"Oh, yeah?" He raised an eyebrow.

We soon arrived at our destination. It could take up to thirty minutes with traffic, but we reached the 34th in just seventeen minutes. On the way, he barely missed hitting at least five pedestrians, three bikes, and four cars.

Just like Federal Plaza, it was a no-frills building with a little touch of dust and mildew.

Rowling went straight to the reception area and informed the officer of the purpose of his visit.

A few minutes later, a middle-aged Latino guy appeared.

"Oh, hell." He grimaced. "Tell me it's a nightmare, or I'm hallucinating."

"Cut it out, Detective Lamont." Rowling snorted. "I thought you'd be excited to see me. Did you forget the last time we saw each other?"

"Of course, I remember. Thanks for reminding

me of a bad memory buried deep in my memory landfill." He shrugged. "What's the deal this time? Are you looking for a demon, shapeshifter, or slit-mouthed woman?"

"I'm here to see John Sangenis, the suspect in the possible murder of Ivan Flynn."

"Oh, that loser. Okay, come on."

He led us to Interrogation Room 6 on the third floor.

A young detective responded to Lamont's knock. At first, he and the other detective didn't look excited about the interruption, but when Lamont stated, "We've got a situation—Rick Rowling," they let us in.

John Sangenis was a good-looking guy; the way he wore his blond hair long reminded me of hair-metal bands around1980s. Perhaps I could have developed a crush on him if it weren't for his voice and the way he spoke.

"Thank God you guys are here to prove my innocence!" he exclaimed.

Immediately, I knew why he wasn't a successful actor.

His posture was bad, his nasally voice was unnaturally high-pitched, and he spoke way too slowly, as if he were stoned or something.

In addition, his gaze was focused on me, which gave me the willies.

"Assuming you're innocent," Rowling chimed in. "Then again, if you're guilty, I'll have you arrested pronto. You understand? Personally, I believe Ivan the lousy painter is already dead."

Considering pelvic bone fragments were left at the scene, along with the dental implant, his claim didn't sound too far-fetched.

Sangenis gasped and squared his shoulders.

"Is he dead? Oh, what a tragic event! What an atrocious destiny!" he over-dramatized.

"What shallow words! What a superficial delivery! What a pathetic excuse for an actor!" was Rick's response. A flicker of annoyance and anger crossed Sangenis's eyes. He looked hard at Rowling.

"You know what, Sam? If you want to make it as an actor, you have to improve your vocabulary and delivery," Rowling, who didn't have the slightest care about the feelings of a crappy actor, declared.

"My name is John!" Sangenis snapped.

He looked more than keen to talk back to Rowling in a fiercer manner, but he stopped short. Maybe he realized it wasn't smart to offend the guy who might prove his innocence. Or maybe it was because of his lack of vocabulary.

Completely ignoring Sangenis's protest, Rowling turned to the detectives. "Can I take a look at the painting found at the scene?"

"Well...." Detective Fender, the older of the detectives, looked unsure at first, but then he nodded. "Okay."

He took us to the evidence room in the basement. Contrary to the ancient looking building, the door of the evidence room was brand new with high-end security.

"There you are." Fender pointed at a canvas. "Guess what? This picture is titled *G.H.O.U.L.*, as in the ghoul. Personally, I'd rather call it *Blank Space* or something like that. The forensics ran chemical and biological tests. They did detect a trace of sagebrush unique to this African island—Cape Verde, but this plant is known to be harmless and assumed to be some kind of additive in the paint. Now take a look at it."

It was an obscure painting colored in dark, depressing shades. A bunch of dead people and soon-to-be victims running for their lives in tattered clothes were drawn at the bottom part of the canvas. Based on this piece of work, I assumed the chances of Ivan Flynn making a huge success in the illustration industry were small.

The nature of the work aside, the most striking part was the blank space, just like Fender mentioned.

There was a huge void shaped like an alpha male on steroids. In this area, the paint was completely missing, and the bare canvas was visible. His arms were raised with his fists clenched, and the muscles in his arms and upper body seemed to be heavily pumped.

Looking at the picture, I recalled a theory in which a giant ghoul came out of the canvas and ate the creator. Of course, I kept my mouth shut. I had read some mystery novels in which the murder victim disappeared like smoke in front of the witnesses. Of course, corpses don't just disappear; the witnesses were tricked into believing the illusion they saw. I was determined *not* to be tricked. I'd had enough insults for one day, and I wasn't keen on becoming the receiving end of further indignation.

Rick Rowling, on the other hand, wasn't as subtle, modest, or hesitant as me.

"All right, here's what happened," he declared. "Apparently, the ghoul in the painting slipped out of the canvas, ate the painter, and went somewhere else."

CHAPTER 6

Detective Fender's facial muscles started twitching as if they had a will of their own. He closed his eyes and took a deep breath, but kept his mouth shut.

I admired the detective's perseverance. Rowling's remark was ridiculous enough to drive a seasoned investigator into yelling at him, or punching him. Perhaps he knew he could shrug off the experience as a weird encounter with an eccentric Fed. On the other hand, I recalled my situation and felt like pulling my hair out. It was day one of my new career as a special assistant in the FBI and—assuming from Hernandez's words—it seemed like I was stuck with this job for a long while. Okay, so it was a free country and I was entitled to leave my position any time I wished. Then again, that didn't mean I could ditch my monstrous student loan.

After a while, Fender groaned through his gritted teeth. "Thank you for identifying the killer."

"You're welcome." Rowling nodded nonchalantly.

"How would you arrest a ghoul? Will there be any judges who'll issue the arrest warrant?" I said. It was meant to be sarcasm, but Rowling didn't get it. On the other hand, Fender's face turned crimson.

"Leave it all to me. For this matter, I need to look at some references to support my theory," Rowling said, and looked at the Patek Philippe watch on his wrist. "Okay, so we'll be back after a lunch break." He turned toward the exit.

I thanked Detective Fender, who responded with a wave. Then I followed my free-spirited boss.

"Hey, have you ever heard of protocol?" I said to Rowling's back.

"Stop talking to me like I'm a barbarian or a Neanderthal. When I was a kid, I was always sent to manners camp. I know how to behave like a responsible, boring adult. It's just that, sometimes, I deliberately avoid behaving like a dull person, mostly because I happen to be a jolly, exciting person."

"Wow, really?" I rolled my eyes.

"Stop rolling your eyes," he reprimanded me without looking back.

"I'm not rolling my eyes," I lied.

Rowling glared at me suspiciously, but proceeded to make a phone call as he continued walking.

Once inside the Ferrari, he got off the phone, and I asked, "What did you mean about the ghoul coming out of the canvas and eating the painter? Sometimes, art pieces are described as lifelike, but usually, such pieces are extremely good. The painting at the station was mediocre at best."

"Yeah, that was mediocre, and the only reason I don't use a stronger word is because it's not worth the criticism." Rowling shrugged.

"Then, what? Don't tell me the paint was made of some kind of flesh-eating bacteria."

"That's close to my theory, if not perfect."

"It was supposed to be a joke."

"Oh, yeah? To be exact, the paint itself was nothing special. But it was laced with a certain kind of microorganism that is kept in an ametabolic state of life, in which an animal's metabolic activities come to a reversible standstill, a.k.a. a temporary and reversible life cessation. These microorganisms were resuscitated with light stimulation, and the rest is history. They proliferated, ate the victim, and as a result, the victim disappeared."

"How can you tell that without running tests?"

"They ran tests and detected a trace of sagebrush from Cape Verde. I have a hunch that the microorganisms that ate Ivan Flynn came from islands close to the African coast." He responded confidently.

"Are you sure such microorganisms exist? Okay, so the mortality rate of flesh-eating bacterial infection tends to be quite high. Then again, it's not like the victims disappear like smoke. Most of the time, the patients get necrotizing fasciitis, sepsis, leading to death by septic shock," I pointed out.

"What do you know about tardigrades?"

I ran a quick search through my memory. During my unfinished medical education, I learned a lot about microorganisms like bacteria, viruses, treponema, parasites, and mycobacteria. "If I recall correctly, they are gross with many legs, and they're not known to cause major infectious diseases."

"Tardigrades—a.k.a. water bears—are water-dwelling, eight-legged, segmented micro-animals about 0.02 inches in length. They're known for being perhaps the most durable of known organisms, able to survive in extreme environments that would kill almost any other animal. For example, they can endure the temperature ranges from minus 458 to 300 degrees Fahrenheit, and more than 1,200 times the normal atmospheric pressure. Throw in ionizing radiation and they can literally breeze out."

With his Formula One-worthy driving

technique, Rowling barely avoided running over a stray goat that wandered into the boulevard. It looked like someone had tried to sacrifice the animal in a Santeria ritual and failed. Considering its track record of survival, it was a truly lucky goat.

"Wow, perhaps they're tougher than roaches."

"Right. They can survive by going into an ametabolic state of life called cryptobiosis. In addition, a class of water bears called Extremus-tardigrada has been reported in a hot spring in Cape Verde, which correlates with the plant trace. Unfortunately, the geographical location where Extremus-tardigrada was originally found, as well as the sample, was destroyed due to an earthquake, and a subsequent search was unsuccessful, so the existence of this class of tardigrade is considered dubious. Then again, multiple cases of missing persons leaving their garments behind before disappearing have been reported in that location."

The car slowed near Yankee Stadium and stopped at a sports bar. Immediately, a drop-dead gorgeous blonde woman in a Diane von Furstenberg wrap dress came out. Air-kissing his cheeks, she cooed, "Hello, darling!"

Then she took an up-and-down glance at me. "Is she a new girlfriend of yours? She's not your usual type, but she's cute, isn't she?" she said, finger-waving at me.

Waving back at her, I responded, "No, I'm an assistant, not a girlfriend." I wanted to tell her Rick Rowling wasn't my type, but I didn't.

"Okay." She nodded and introduced herself as Jamie.

"What is your problem?" Rowling raised an eyebrow at me. "Most women react with a blush or something that implies they are happy, excited, or euphoric."

"I'm not most women."

"That explains your terrible taste in men." He snorted.

"Excuse me? What do you know about my taste in men?"

Without answering my question, he countered, "What do *you* find irresistible in a man?"

"That's a good question." I wanted to say it was none of his business, but I refrained. "I appreciate a guy who is strong, but also gentle, who can be serious and funny at appropriate times. Someone who is intelligent, thoughtful, and a good listener. He must be comfortable being both the leader and the follower, secure enough to accept me just as I am, and love me no matter what, in spite of sickness, human failings, and unnatural or abnormal deaths."

"Ha. The man with the traits of your preference exists only in really lame romance novels. On the other hand, the most eligible bachelor in Manhattan happens to be standing in front of you."

"Oh, yeah? Where is he? Is he invisible or something?" I shot back.

"Technically, he's Mr. Number Two of the most eligible bachelors," Jamie chimed in.

Shushing her with a flip of his hand, Rowling shook his head. "Mandy, you must be blind. When was the last time you had your vision checked?"

"My vision is perfect, thank you very much," I assured him. "By the way, being elected as one of the most eligible bachelors is wonderful. Then again, bragging about it seems somewhat, you know, pathetic?"

"Did you just call me pathetic?" He narrowed his eyes. "Answer carefully, Mandy. I can fire you right here, right now."

"No, I didn't!" I denied profusely. "I was talking hypothetically." As much as I hated this job, I *really* didn't want to be fired. Having been expelled from medical school was bad enough, but getting fired on the first day of my new job would be downright disastrous.

Jamie cleared her throat. "You guys coming inside, or what?"

"Of course we're coming inside," Rowling grunted.

Jamie led us into the establishment. White linen tablecloths and the classic wood interior weren't what I expected in a sports bar. The place was full of patrons, and we were taken to the private room in the innermost part.

As soon as we were seated, Rowling said, "As usual, I'll have a ribeye steak with a side of fries."

"Okay. What about you?"

"Well, let me see…." I studied the menu with perhaps more intensity and diligence than I usually displayed during exams. Did I mention I enjoy food? I was torn between crab cakes, shrimp scampi, and shrimp cocktail. Then I noticed they had Kobe beef sliders.

"Mandy, are you going to spend the entire lunch time moaning?" Rowling inquired. "Order whatever you want. I'll pay the bill."

"Really? Thanks. Okay, I'll have Kobe beef sliders and a shrimp cocktail."

Rowling rolled his eyes.

"Alrighty," Jamie said in a singsong voice.

When she left, Rowling started reading an e-book on a tablet device.

After a while of intense reading, he said, "Okay, I've got everything covered."

"Did you find any incidents about human-eating painting materials?" I asked.

"Yes." He nodded.

"Seriously? Assuming such cases exist, the news and the Internet should be all over human-eating paints."

"Except the TV and Internet didn't exist back in the sixteenth century. Want to take a look?" He offered me the tablet.

I looked at the title page. "Is it in Spanish?"

"Yes. The title in English would be something like *Ye Olde Tales of India and Witchcraft*."

"Okay, so the setting of this book is in India." I had no idea why he was using a book about old tales as a reference, but I decided to play along and enjoy my lunch.

"Not the India in the Asian continent. The book refers to the North and South American continents that Columbus mistook as India. What do you know about Spanish history in the sixteenth century?"

"Sixteenth century? Isn't that when *Pirates of the Caribbean* was set?"

"No, the movie series is set in the eighteenth century. Anything else you know about the historical events in the sixteenth century?"

"I don't know. They were cruising in big vessels. I think big vessels like the ones departing from the Port of Miami nowadays. Royal Caribbean, Princess, Disney, you name it."

"Is that a joke?" Rowling furrowed his eyebrows.

"You know what? I'm not much into history. In my opinion, history is a novel with no taste, written by the people who claimed victory over those who had lesser say."

"I understand you suck at history."

"I was good at art history. Looking at all the lovely pottery, paintings, and sculptures was absolutely fascinating. On the other hand, I had no interest in general history. All the battles, wars, treaties, and politics were boring. They were just old events with similar, boring names. Perhaps if history textbooks were written in the same style and voice as the *New York Post*, they would be more readable."

"Okay, cut it out. I should have skipped the backstory." Rowling rubbed his temples.

The food came and we started eating.

Cutting up his juicy and delicious-looking ribeye steak, Rowling said, "Basically, the sixteenth century was the prime time for Spain and Portugal, exploring the world's seas, opening world-wide oceanic trade routes, and colonizing large parts of Mundo Nuevo, a.k.a. the New World. The Portuguese became the masters of Asia's and Africa's Indian Ocean trade, and the Spanish took a large part of the Americas. Back in that time, the economy was literally booming in those areas. It is said that approximately five tons of gold and three hundred tons of silver went across the Atlantic Ocean directly to Spain from Central and South America each year. Thanks to the enslavement of the native people, forcing them to work without pay, it was a business with super-efficient profitability. Thus, a humongous wealth went to Spain. Meanwhile, thanks to the endless influx of said wealth, the people in Spain stopped working, which suddenly degraded the general labor ethics among them. The Jewish replaced the Spaniards in labor forces, and eventually, they took over the world of finances."

I listened while munching on one of the large shrimp. I didn't dare interrupt his story by asking things like, 'What does that have to do with human-eating microorganisms?' because I was getting keen on knowing more about the story.

Snatching a shrimp from my plate, he continued. "There's a chapter about this villain called Alejandro Tremellius, a Spanish colonel who served in the New World as the manager of a gold mine for five years. He did a great job for the government of Spain in the New World, meaning he made the natives' lives a living hell.

"Tremellius was a typical villain who had appeared in many stories like *Grimm's Fairy Tales*. He was greedy, sadistic, and evil, yet he knew how to sweeten up with the powerful. He was such a common villain that he couldn't have had his name in the book if it weren't for his sudden disappearance in the year 1547 from his home in Toledo.

"When he disappeared, Tremellius was a wealthy retiree. After his successful deployment in the New World, he landed a new career in the maintenance of the public order back home in Spain. Again, he did an outstanding job, taking care of the Protestant movement by forcibly suppressing the mob of humans. In addition, he literally made a killing during the procedure by making false accusations of conspiracy on several innocent Jews. He employed intense torturing, and he didn't let them go until they paid him handsomely.

"According to the book, he knew how the Protestants, the Jews, and the native peoples loathed him, but he didn't seem bothered by such feelings like regret and remorse. At home, he was a loving father and husband. In his retirement, art was his new passion, and he was determined to have great success as a painter. He was set on taking a victory over the El Greco, who was the 'it' painter in that time and probably one of the most well-known artists in history."

"Outshining the El Greco? Seriously?" I muttered.

"Tremellius's ambition sounds like a joke here in the twenty-first century, but he lived in the sixteenth century, and he was serious.

"Indeed, it is recorded in this book that he wasn't a bad painter. His paintings were good, except they were not as striking or sensational as those of El Greco's. He was a strong sympathizer of hostile art critics against the acclaimed painter living in the same city.

"Tremellius worked hard. He had achieved moderate success, but the gap between El Greco and him was getting even bigger. Frustrated, he blamed paints, brushes, and canvases. He blinded one of his servants by poking him in the eye with a brush, which helped Tremellius's already bad reputation nose-dive. As a result, he grew even more aggressive."

And Rowling's story reached its climax....

"One day, an old Jewish man knocked on his door. He told Tremellius that he was a merchant and a huge fan of his art.

"His compliment earned him an opportunity to pitch his product to Tremellius. The man said to Tremellius, 'Our enterprise has just acquired the most fascinating and mystical painting material from a Portuguese merchant. This material was extracted from a particular kind of moss existing in the crater of the most deadly active volcano from the deepest part of Africa. Have you ever seen the Kano school of Japanese painting? Indeed, some of the greatest masters of this school used this material to create spectacular paintings. The Japanese named this product Busu and, even in Japan, only a chosen few artists have access to it. All you need to do is mix the material with your paint and work on your masterpiece. Busu responds to light stimuli, and starts pulsating with the paint. This response gives amazing effects to your already great masterpiece, making your art even more animated and sensational than ever.'"

  I could almost hear the Jewish guy pitching.

  "Back then, paintings from Japan were hot among the European art society. According to the book, Tremellius was always enthusiastic about trying new painting material. Indeed, he might have been willing to employ even the darkest power of Lucifer if there were even the smallest chance of defeating El Greco.

  "Still, Tremellius put on a skeptical façade. 'How would I know if you're telling the truth? Then again, your tale was intriguing. Though my talent as an artist isn't something affected by painting materials, I can always try new products. Leave all of this new paint. I'll try it first and consider paying for it later.'

  "'I'm awfully sorry, sir, but I'm afraid I cannot do that. Actually, half of what I have here is reserved for Señor El Greco. You know, the price is not too high, but a promise is a promise.'

  "The price quote he reluctantly gave to Tremellius as the deal with El Greco was as much as the average annual salary of an upper-class bureaucrat.

"'I'll pay twice as much as that. Leave the paint already!' Tremellius almost snatched it from the merchant. True to his words, he paid the full price in cash, though he didn't forget to say, 'If this paint turns out to be fake, I'll find you, kill you, and let the pigs eat your flesh. You understand?'

"Using the 'magical' paint, Tremellius started working on a new project named *The Dark Trinity*, in which he had planned to portray Lucifer as the son. Withdrawn in his atelier, he even banned his family from contacting him while he worked.

"The only person who was permitted to come near him during this time period was his servant of thirty years. He delivered meals to the atelier's door twice each day.

"On the thirtieth night, the servant delivered dinner to his master's atelier. Upon leaving, he caught a joyous shriek from Tremellius.

"'*Dios mio!* It's true…. He is moving! Lucifer's whole body is pulsating as if he is about to come to life! I can't wait to have this work evaluated by the critics! Look at Lucifer, his evilness… it's completely different from the other parts I had painted with regular paint. I must admit that this new product is groundbreaking, giving an absolute contrast between justice and immorality.'

"Those turned out to be the final words of Tremellius.

"The next day, the servant came to the atelier as usual to deliver breakfast and fetch the dinner tray. What was unusual was that the food was untouched.

"The servant notified the family. After a heated discussion, and weighing the pros and cons of paying a visit to the atelier, they broke down the door. Inside, a large canvas stood on the easel in the center of the room. Scattered on the floor were the paints, palettes, brushes, and the garments; however, Alejandro Tremellius was nowhere to be seen.

"When they took a look at the canvas, the piece of artwork seemed quite unusual. The background was painted in complex dark tones, and the Holy Spirit and the Father were drawn and painted. But what appeared to be Lucifer as the son was nothing but a huge, body-shaped blank space."

CHAPTER 7

"Then what? Did they find the killer?" I asked.

"Of course not," he said matter-of-factly. "I didn't exist in the sixteenth century."

"Uh-huh" was my response. I was getting used to his presumptuous attitude.

"Uh-huh? That's all you have to say?" He frowned.

"In addition, thanks for a lovely lunch." I smiled, sipping a nice cup of peppermint tea. "The Kobe beef sliders were very yummy, and the shrimp…. They were just divine."

"Okay. Anyway, based on the way Flynn disappeared, the possibility of Extremus-tardigrada— a.k.a. Busu—being the murder weapon is pretty high. In addition, this book hasn't been translated into English, so we can narrow the suspects to those who can read Spanish."

"Wow, so we have only forty-five million suspects in the nation!" I said. "Not to mention that anyone can download the e-book."

"Fortunately, the number of suspects is pretty limited." Rowling made a swiping move with his right index finger, telling me the book was only available in hardcover edition. The only reason he had the e-book version was because USCAB happened to be a major developer in the e-book industry, and most of the books he called references had been converted into e-books just for him.

According to him, they were old books and copyright wasn't an issue.

Rowling put his empty coffee cup on the table. "Let's go back to the NYPD."

Ten minutes later, we were back in the interrogation room at the 34th Precinct, where John Sangenis was being held.

I could tell how unhappy Detective Fender was from his facial expression, but of course, Rowling didn't care.

"Stop playing a game and just admit that you murdered Ivan Flynn," Rowling told Sangenis.

"Oh, what an irrational guess. What a terrible interrogation. Talk about a false accusation," Sangenis responded in a flat voice.

"Hmm, that was better than the last time, in that you didn't squawk. Still, you're far from being a decent actor."

Following Rowling's sarcastic remark, Sangenis snarled, "What about you? For a decent investigator, you're doing nothing but making a groundless accusation against me. You're not following protocol, and you have no evidence. I don't know how you can live with that."

"That's not an issue for me. I'm not a decent investigator." Rowling shrugged.

"Wow, you can be quite modest if you try. I'm surprised!" Sangenis threw his hands in the air.

Rowling responded with a one-eyebrow raise. "Don't get me wrong. I meant to say that I'm a phenomenal investigator and not a decent investigator, which allows me to skip the menial order of procedures."

Sangenis's jaw dropped; he was at a loss for words. I was standing by the door, trying to be as invisible as possible. In addition, by being close to the exit, I could run.

Detective Fender stage-whispered to me, "Are you sure it's okay to let him have his way?"

"What do *you* think?" I asked. "No offense, but I suppose you're much more familiar with dealing with him than I am. Actually, today happens to be my first day working with him, and I'm quite lost here."

Fender shut his eyes, clenched his fists, and took a deep breath.

Immediately, I regretted saying that. Obviously, my response wasn't something he wanted to hear. I was afraid he would start yelling at me like a temperamental attending physician, but he didn't. Instead, he said, "I don't know how you ended up in your position, but I'm sorry."

I was touched. Actually, I almost cried. Fender had just told me the nicest thing I'd heard in months. During my days in clinical rotations, the majority of attending physicians were evil and mean-spirited. They yelled at me, pushed me around, and humiliated me whenever possible. I was called a moron at times when I couldn't give them the right answer, and also when I *did* come up with the right answer but they were hoping I'd screw up. I got used to being the recipient of verbal and psychological abuse to the point that I always prepared myself for being treated badly. It was unbelievably fabulous to know that not all people were malevolent.

"Thank you very much, Detective Fender," I said, sniffing a little.

"It's okay. Compared to the last time, he's behaving. I guess you have a good influence on him."

"You think so?"

Meanwhile, Rowling was still talking to John

Sangenis, but I was too busy befriending the detective and wasn't paying much attention to my boss. In addition, his voice had dropped, so I couldn't hear him very clearly.

Still, I caught Sangenis retorting, "What the hell are you talking about? Can't you at least try speaking in a language I can understand?"

Arms crossed, Rowling stared at the wannabe actor, but he didn't say a word.

Precisely at that moment, Sangenis's lawyer appeared, requesting the 34th Precinct release her client immediately.

"I'm leaving. I'm totally sick of playing along with your little game. If you want to have a conversation with me, I recommend getting a warrant next time!" Snarling, Sangenis stood.

Detectives Fender and Lamont clenched their fists.

"We will," Lamont said through gritted teeth. "See you soon."

"By the way," Sangenis turned to Rowling, "does it make you feel good about yourself when you judge people as if you're the supreme justice?"

"Of course I feel good about what I do," Rowling declared. "Are you implying there are better things to do in life? If so, I'm more than happy to hear that."

Then it was Sangenis's turn to shut up.

Grinning like a cat licking cream, Rowling added, "Anyway, keep barking all you want. You won't last long anyway."

"I will file a formal complaint against all of you here for police brutality and a violation of human rights, and I'll sue you like hell. So be prepared," Sangenis spat before he turned on his heels and left, flashing a victorious smile.

It was John Sangenis's one minute of victory. Actually, it was his final moment of triumph because, later that day, he disappeared from the surface of the Earth.

As in literally.

The police couldn't keep Sangenis in custody; however, that didn't mean they gave up catching him for good.

When he went back to his apartment in Brooklyn, a couple of detectives from the 34th Precinct followed. Luckily, there was a grocery store in front of the building where Sangenis lived, making it easy for the detectives to conduct surveillance on the target. Plus, both his unit and the entrance to the building were clearly visible from the parking lot. Indeed, it was an ideal building for a stakeout, for it had no back door.

As it grew darker, the detectives saw the light flickering in Sangenis's window on the third floor. Behind the curtain, they could see the movement of a silhouette.

At first, there was little activity in the apartment as they watched the silhouette sitting, standing, and coming in and out of their vision.

A van with 'Bobby's Movin' Diner' written on both sides stopped in front of the building, and a guy in a uniform carrying a Styrofoam container went inside, came out, and then left.

The light was still on at a few minutes past midnight, and for the first time, there was a major move behind the curtain.

In front of the detectives' eyes, the human-shaped silhouette of John Sangenis started bouncing up and down. It turned and twisted while wiggling and jumping, and then it dropped to the floor.

At first, they wondered if the target was practicing hip-hop, freestyle dance moves, but all of a sudden, the fast-paced movements stopped.

While the detectives shook their heads in confusion, wondering if the target was trying to provoke them, they heard the dispatcher on the radio saying there was a noise complaint at the apartment they were watching.

According to the dispatcher, neighbors on the second floor heard a series of earsplitting screams.

When they entered the apartment, there was no sign of life.

In the room facing the parking lot, the detectives discovered clothes and shoes scattered on the floor, which they positively identified as the garments John Sangenis was wearing when they saw him last. Also, an empty bottle of ketchup and an empty Styrofoam container were scattered on the floor. Strangely, both the bottle and container were completely clear of condiment or food particles, as if they were washed and cleaned. Just like the night of Ivan Flynn's disappearance, a candle was blazing.

Considering Sangenis couldn't get out of the building without being seen by the detectives, they had no choice but to come to the conclusion that he had disappeared from his apartment.

But they couldn't figure out *how*. Even more confounding was why he'd used a giant candle in the well-lit room.

CHAPTER 8

While the detectives from the 34th Precinct were hard at surveying John Sangenis, I was having a problem of my own.

Rick Rowling decided it was a good idea to home-deliver me to my parents' townhouse in the suburb of Queens. I declined his offer politely, but he didn't listen.

"You know, you'll be disappointed. It's a no-frills, boring suburb with nothing interesting to see," I warned Rowling while riding shotgun in the Ferrari. "And the house is small."

"Sounds very interesting," he said nonchalantly. "As a resident of Fifth Avenue, visiting a little house in the suburbs is good for a change."

When we crossed into the neighborhood casually referred to as 'the hood,' my phone chirped.

"Hello?"

As soon as I took the call, Nana's chipper voice jumped into my left ear. "Guess what, Mandy? Mrs. Luciano just called me, and she says she saw a flashy Ferrari speeding through the town."

"Oh, really?" I responded. I didn't know what else to say.

"Yup. Then again, her vision's not so clear due to cataracts and everything, so I'm pretty much skeptical," she said. "By the way, where are you?"

"I'm close to home. Will be there in, say, three minutes." I looked out the window. It should have been the same old view, but this time, it felt like

I had wandered into *The Twilight Zone*.

"Good. Don't be late. Today's dinner will be meatloaf, and it won't be good when it's cold. Look out for the Ferrari and take a photo if you can, okay?" Nana said, and she hung up.

"Ciao," I said to the silent phone, and turned to Rowling. "Hey, Rick, guess what? Mrs. Luciano has called everyone in the neighborhood about a flashy Ferrari. I guess the whole town's talking about you."

"Hmm, no problem." He pushed on the gas.

A minute later, we came to a skidding stop at the driveway of my parents' townhouse.

Nana and Mom were outside, probably waiting for me. Nana was from my mother's side of the family, and she had been living with my parents since Granddad passed away three years ago. She resided in the room that used to be my younger sister Alicia's. Good thing she was happily married to a corporate lawyer in L.A.; otherwise, I'd have to share my room with Nana. I loved her, but she snores like a locomotive. Anyway, I had yet to be accustomed to the hustle and bustle of living with my folks. I really needed space.

When I crawled out of the Ferrari, trying my best not to puke, Rowling was already shaking hands with them. And before I had a chance to make an intervention, Rick Rowling was invited to dinner at my parents' place.

In an attempt to scare my boss off, I warned him, "You know what? They're not serving Kobe beef, not even grass-fed Angus beef. Are you sure you'd like to eat commoner food in the commoner neighborhood?"

"For your information, I'm a commoner, just

like you," he responded matter-of-factly.

"Guess what? Nana's Italian and my mother's half-Romanian and half-Italian, and they'll ask you a lot of personal questions. Especially Nana. She's nosy. If there's anyone nosier than her, it's Mrs. Luciano, who lives in a house three blocks behind our lane."

"What about your father?" He cocked his head to the side.

"He's polite but awkward. Guess what? He's British."

"Then I see no problem." He flashed his perfect set of pearly whites.

And there I was, sitting at the table set for five, feeling as awkward and surreal as ever.

Actually, surreal was a better word to describe my perception than the reality, which was impossible and unthinkable. Things were not going very conventionally. Usually, you didn't get delivered to your parents and grandma in your boss's Ferrari, or eat two meals of the day with your boss. Then throw in the fact that your grandma was taking selfies in the driver's seat and on the rooftop of said Ferrari. Talk about wickedness!

Indeed, everything was so out of the ordinary, I was either in a bizarre daydream or out of my mind.

While I busied myself with escapism, I caught Mom saying, "Would you like more mashed potatoes, Rick?"

"Yes, please. Thank you, Mrs. Meyer." Rowling smiled. Against my speculations, he was acting like a pleasant gentleman. I wondered why he couldn't behave himself during the job, where he could be a man of honor.

"What a lovely evening!" Nana said, grinning

ear to ear. "We're so pleased to have you here, Rick. You should come more often."

"Thank you very much, Mrs. Moretti. I'm so happy to work with a person from such a nice family."

"Oh no, Rick, you can call me Leonora."

"Great, Leonora. Nice meeting you."

Before I knew it, Rowling was on a first-name basis with Nana.

"Are you married?" Nana asked abruptly.

"No, I'm single."

"That's great, isn't it?" said Nana. "Mandy here is single as well. She used to be engaged to a doctor, but he died."

"If I remember correctly, he's not dead," Dad corrected. He wasn't a chatty guy, but he had this tendency with accuracy. Perhaps it had something to do with him being an accountant.

"He's as good as dead," Nana retorted. "I put the dreaded Romanian eye on that heartless, gutless, spineless bastard. His whole body will swell up and turn into a pukey shade of puce, and then kaboom! He's a dead man. He deserves to die, walking away from his fiancée like that."

I groaned. I really, *really* hated when they reminded me of Justin, especially in front of guests—above all, in front of Rick Rowling. So I did what I could—I pretended not to be listening.

"Mother! We're at the table and have a guest!" Mom snapped. "In addition, everybody dies, eventually. Oh, and don't even think about my baby being accused of being the Grim Reaper!" My mother, of all people, announced my biggest taboo.

I wished to drop dead on the spot, just to save myself from the misery of living. Obviously, Rowling was gathering enough information to pick on me until the day of my retirement.

While I was seriously weighing the pros and cons of slashing my gut with a dinner knife, Nana said, "What are we having for dessert?"

"Pineapple upside-down cake" was Mom's response.

My ears perked up. I loved pineapple upside-down cake. Okay, so I could commit *hara-kiri* after dessert.

After an hour of additional agony, dinner was over.

When Rowling thanked my folks and stood to leave, carrying leftovers, I followed him out the door, just to be polite. If I didn't need to be polite, I'd have snatched the leftovers, curled up in the corner of my room, and drank my sorrows away with cold meatloaf and mashed potatoes on the side. It's common knowledge that leftovers are the yummiest part of the dinner, and I didn't like the fact that my brand new boss got them.

"Don't say I didn't warn you about my dysfunctional family," I said.

"Dysfunctional? Your family?" A corner of his mouth lifted. "After all, there was no bloodbath during the meal. You should see mine to get an idea of a dysfunctional family." He didn't seem to be kidding.

"Wow," I replied.

"By the way, Mandy." He looked me in the eye. "Do you want him dead?"

"Him? Who? What are you talking about?"

"Justin, your ex-fiancé," he said nonchalantly. "If you'd like, I can have him killed, make his death look like a totally innocent accident. People often die of freak accidents, such as—"

"Too much information!" I covered my ears with my hands. "And no, thanks. You don't need to have him…. You know what," I added hurriedly. Okay, so technically, I often fantasized about my ex-fiancé dropping dead by stumbling on the wet operation room floor and stabbing himself with the scalpel. Then again, it seemed like having Rick Rowling's help in hiring a contract killer came with a huge price tag.

"Hmm, okay." He nodded, loading the leftover meatloaf and mashed potatoes on the passenger's seat. "Remember, you can always change your mind."

I thought a little, and said, "Thank you for the offer."

"No prob." He shrugged. "Hey, the doctor guy's not worth your time."

"What do you know about him?" I asked.

"He's a self-centered, no good, arrogant asshole."

"I know." I chuckled.

"In addition, he's deep in debt up to his eyeballs following a screw-up in options trading. His desperate attempt to recover the loss by scoring big in Vegas completely backfired. Obviously, card counting isn't one of his strong suits. Anyway, even his family has cut him off."

"How do you know that?"

"Do you really want to know how I got the info?" He raised an eyebrow.

"No," I replied. "I was just saying."

For a brief moment, we fell silent.

"Thanks for dinner," Rowling said finally.

When I was about to say "It was nice having

you over," he cupped my face and kissed me lightly. On. The. Lips.

I knew I could have resisted, and I should have, but I didn't.

It was just a brush of a kiss, but still deep enough to make me want for more.

"Good night." He climbed into the Ferrari and drove away.

"Good night." I stood outside until the taillights faded in the night.

CHAPTER 9

The next day was Saturday, and I slept late. I was planning to spend the rest of the day lazily, but then I got a phone call from Detective Fender.

"He disappeared!" he announced. "John Sangenis disappeared from his own apartment in front of two detectives on a stakeout!"

He told me to call Rick Rowling, sounding happy. When I asked him why, he said, "That's because you're the one responsible for calling him, not me." Then it dawned on me why the detective was so keen on exchanging phone numbers, saying, "Just in case of progress or a situation."

Shaking my head, I called Rowling, who answered on the second ring.

"I knew he wasn't the killer," he said, yawning. "You saw how he responded when I dissed him in Spanish in the interrogation room, didn't you? Considering he totally stank as an actor, it's plausible to assume the guy didn't understand the language, especially from the sixteenth century."

I recalled the previous day's events. Though at that moment, I was busy chatting with Detective Fender, I caught John Sangenis saying something about trying to speak in a language he could understand. I finally realized he meant it literally, not rhetorically.

"So, who is the killer?" I mumbled.

"It's simple. Ruth MacMahon is our killer."

"Ruth MacMahon? As in John's girlfriend?"

"Yup, as in the girl who dated not just one but two losers."

"Are you sure?"

"Of course. The father of the MacMahon sisters used to be an ambassador, and they used to travel a lot in their youth, including many Spanish-speaking countries like Spain, Argentina, Mexico, and Peru. In addition, she's taken multiple trips to Cape Verde in the past three months."

The part about Cape Verde sounded perfectly convincing, even to me, except for a tiny issue.

"Still, what's the motive for offing the boyfriends?" I questioned. "Okay, assuming Ivan Flynn was as dim-witted as John Sangenis, I can easily imagine Ruth getting sick of them. Then again, she could have just broken up with them."

"I think she wanted to tidy up around herself."

"By killing them? For what purpose? Was she meeting a new guy?" I muttered. "No, she's been two-timing those boys. She could always three-time."

"Actually, she happens to be one of those hardcore, corporate-type women." Rowling snorted. "She's just joined USCAB and will be starting at the West Coast branch in L.A. in a month. That said, it wouldn't be over the top to assume she decided to eliminate the worthless guys with larger-than-life egos before they started messing with her new career and potential success."

Listening to his words, I recalled the way Justin ditched me like a gallstone because standing up for me or sticking by me was bad for his career. "That's cruel!" I felt like crawling in the corner of the room and crying away my sorrows.

Before I started sobbing, Rowling's chuckle from the other end of the line dragged me back to reality. "Hmm, it looks like my strategy has worked nice and smooth."

"What do you mean?"

"I knew Ruth would screw up if I accused Sangenis of the murder of Flynn, which makes it appear as if she's off the suspects list."

"Excuse me? Does that mean you were accusing a totally innocent guy yesterday?"

"Yep. At that time, it seemed like a good idea. You admitted he was an asshole, didn't you?" he responded.

"That doesn't entitle you to make a false accusation!"

"I know," he said. "So, I'm going to close this case instantaneously to make amends. Look, Mandy, a driver will pick you up in five minutes, so get dressed."

Then he disconnected.

Twenty minutes later, I was delivered to a condo building in Midtown, the home of Ruth MacMahon. It was an elegant, upscale place, but I wasn't feeling strong enough to be impressed or envious.

Actually, I was glad I'd been delivered in one piece. The driver Rowling mentioned came to pick me up on a monstrous Harley-Davidson. As a suburban girl, I was accustomed to riding shotgun in a minivan, not a Harley. And reaching the destination in fifteen minutes instead of thirty, as suggested by Google Maps, might appeal to some people, but it was a traumatic journey for me. In addition, the biker guy, named Hawk, was a huge alpha male with way too much of his body covered in tattoos. I was almost compelled to ask him if he'd ever heard of contracting Hepatitis-B during tattoo procedures, but

I was busy trying my best not to pee myself.

"Hey, Hawk, you're one minute late," Rowling, who was leaning on his parked Ferrari, remarked.

"Sorry, Head," said Hawk in his raspy voice. "I had to make a brief stop for Miz Meyer so she could take a moment to recover. You wouldn't be happy if she was dead due to suffocation by vomit, would you?"

"Good point." Rowling nodded. "I appreciate your work. Now you can go."

"Any time you need my service." The biker flashed white, straight teeth and left with the engine roaring.

"I didn't know he worked for the FBI," I said.

"He doesn't." Rowling shook his head. "Hawk is the president of a motorcycle club called Devils of Anarchy, and he's not affiliated with the Feds."

"Devils of Anarchy?" My eyes grew wide. My eyeballs would have popped out, rolling on the ground like a pair of bouncy balls, if it were a cartoon and not my life. "Isn't that an outlaw bikers' club with a long rap sheet of criminal allegations?" Then I recalled Hawk called Rowling 'Head.' "Are you a member of that club?"

"No, I'm not." He shrugged. "You're asking because he called me Head, right?"

"Yes."

"That's so lame, and I've repeatedly told him to stop calling me that, but he always forgets. That meathead. Officially, I have no affiliation with the club. It's just that Hawk likes doing errands for me." When I continued staring at him incredulously, he continued. "Okay, so it's true they took some part in several criminal allegations and incidents in the past, but now they've reformed." He shrugged.

"How did the president of a notorious outlaw bikers' club end up running errands for you?"

"If I tell you that, I'd have to kill you." He winked. "Let's go catch our killer."

When Rowling beeped Ruth MacMahon on the intercom from the entrance hall, she told him it was not a good time for a visitor, as she was going out. However, she buzzed us in when he mentioned the part about John Sangenis's death. Technically, it was just a disappearance, since his body hadn't been discovered, but I wasn't going to let this fact become the point of an argument. Considering the metal implants that should be in his body were found at the scene of his disappearance, it seemed like enough to presume he was dead as well. With or without the corpses, it didn't make this case any more bizarre.

When I set foot into Ruth's unit, I was impressed. The foyer was grand, the marble floor gleaming. The décor was stylish modern, with furniture from name brands such as a sofa from Cassina and an unbelievably beautiful coffee table from Creazioni. It seemed as if her place had popped out of some super-luxurious interior design magazine. In the depth of the room, one side of the wall consisted of a huge floor-to-ceiling window, overlooking Central Park. I felt almost compelled to take a selfie, with the window and the park beneath as the background. The place looked like a paradise for someone hoping to score killer selfies.

Rick Rowling, on the other hand, wasn't impressed at all.

Ruth was sitting on the sofa, dressed in a smart little black dress, looking delicate yet stunningly beautiful. When she invited us to sit down,

Rowling declined her offer, to my disappointment. I was tempted to sit on all the beautiful chairs to see which ones I liked. So I was deep in debt—that didn't mean I had completely given up on getting rich. I could always score a jackpot in Powerball.

"I apologize for your inconvenience," he said, smiling. "Indeed, I feel really bad about interrupting your project after you have gone so far as to kill your loser boyfriends. I'd be really pissed if I were you."

"I don't know what you're talking about." Ruth furrowed her perfectly sculpted eyebrows.

"By the way, I have some urgent business lined up, so I have to close this case within a couple of hours. Okay, so you're a much better actor than the late John Sangenis. Then again, you're not worth spending my precious time on. Luckily for you, the state of New York doesn't offer the death penalty, so why don't you just fess up to make my job easier?"

Even to me, Rowling's demand was way over the top, and Ruth responded to him with a snort. "Well, well, well. They say the apple doesn't fall too far from the tree, but sometimes, I'm afraid this saying turns out to be incorrect."

"I'll take that as a compliment. Now, fess up."

"Even if you say so, I have nothing to confess." Ruth shrugged. "By the way, could I ask you one thing?"

"Go ahead."

"How could you be so certain about your unfounded accusation against me? What do you know about the alleged murders?"

"M.O. and the motive are what I know."

"Okay, so tell me about this alleged M.O."

"You used temporarily inactivated tardigrades as the weapon of both murders. To off Ivan Flynn, you handed him a tube of paint laced with tardigrades that were activated with light stimuli. With John, your tactic was a little bit more complicated. You put the ketchup laced with tardigrades in his fridge. I don't know when you slipped the ketchup, but you had opportunities. To ensure that John would be gone in no time, you called up Bobby's Movin' Diner to have a hotdog and French fries delivered. In addition, when John called to thank you, you told him to use ketchup. That was subtle. Oh, by the way, John's phone was tapped."

"Says you." She chuckled. "Then again, maybe those alleged murders have only happened in your head. I also think it's impossible to prove, especially when you don't have the corpses. Besides, leaving ketchup in my boyfriend's fridge, telling him about how delicious this specialty ketchup makes the food is completely innocent, isn't it?"

When she said that, I sensed something evil, which didn't fit her delicate façade.

"NYPD is in charge of building a case, and prosecuting is the district attorney's job. Actually, I don't really care if they suffer while doing their jobs or not, because it's none of my business. What I'm concerned about is you." Rowling looked directly in Ruth's eyes.

"Oh, really? Am I supposed to be flattered? Though, isn't it a little kinky to be involved with the son of my own sister's lover?"

"Come on, that's not what I mean. I have standards." Now it was Rowling's turn to snort. "Let me get this straight. I don't really care if you offed your two loser boyfriends. Still, you seem to be overzealous, and I've got to nip your ambition in the bud before you eliminate your sister using the same method and replace her position as Miss Tuesday."

Ruth took a deep breath.

I looked at her, and then at Rowling. Okay, his words made sense. Ruth wasn't a baby's breath at all. She would *kill* to build a successful career at USCAB, and even I could tell sleeping with the CEO would help a lot when it came to climbing up the corporate ladder. Also, considering Rowling's father was widowed, she could aim for an even higher position, such as Mrs. CEO.

"That's the most ridiculous thing I've ever heard. You must be delusional." Ruth giggled.

"You know what? Your sister didn't laugh when I told her my opinion," Rowling said nonchalantly.

Ruth's mouth was still open, but her voice wasn't audible anymore.

"Before coming here, I made a call to Beth," Rowling continued. "Of course, she likes her current position as Miss Tuesday for my old man. Not to mention she has no suicidal ideation either. And guess what? She told me about the package you sent from Cape Verde. Beth was the initial recipient, but you picked it up from her place as soon as you were back in the city. She has her share of curiosity, of course, and she took a peek inside the package. So you told her it was dried plants, but she got nervous when she saw a white powder-like substance. She was concerned, so she took a small sample of the material, just as a precaution. Now it looks like her precaution's paying off, isn't it, Ruth? She had already turned in the sample for an assessment."

Ruth's lips quivered, but no words came out.

CHAPTER 10

With a weird moan, her whole body shivering, Ruth MacMahon collapsed onto the sofa.

Considering the floor was made of marble, she was lucky she was already sitting on the sofa when she crumpled. If she were standing, she might have ended up banging her head on the floor.

"Oh, my God, is she dead?" I gasped.

She was lying there, totally motionless. One elbow was stiffly bent at a right angle, as if she were turned into stone as the result of looking Medusa in the eye.

"Try touching her, Mandy. What do you say about taking her pulse?" Rowling said, grinning ear-to- ear.

"That's not funny, Rick!" I snapped.

"For your information, I'm not trying to be funny. I always wanted to see an evil killer dropping dead in front of me. That'll save us a whole lot of trouble, you know."

I smacked him on the shoulder.

"Ouch! Hey, I didn't ask you to whack me," he protested.

"You're still breathing." I snorted. "Now, it's official: I'm not the Grim Reaper. If I were, you'd be dead by now. I doubt you're all pure and innocent."

"You don't understand. Hey, why can't you see me as an honest-to-God, righteous, and flawless justice in shining armor? Mandy, you really need to have your eyes checked." He leaned over and touched

Ruth's neck. "Hmm, she's alive." Looking bored, Rowling took two pairs of handcuffs out of his jacket pocket.

"Wow, that's a relief," I said, and I meant it.

"Oh, yeah? It's just a conversion disorder. Beth told me Ruth manifests this symptom when she's put under stress." Leaving Ruth, now with her hands and legs secured in handcuffs, on the sofa, Rowling cocked his head. "Let's call it a day and leave this place."

"Excuse me?" My eyes widened.

"I said, let's leave this boring place. I don't care about all the mumbo jumbo of making arrests, prosecuting, and taking cases to trial. Now that we've gotten the situation under control, let's call it a day and leave the mess for agents covering violent crimes, or the NYPD. I'm way too busy to be bothered by such a minor issue," Rowling declared and turned on his heels to leave the condo.

"Excuse me, Rick," I called to his back.

"What?" he asked without turning around.

"We can't just leave," I said. Then it suddenly occurred to me that offending my boss furthermore wasn't in my best interest, so I added, "I'm afraid."

"Why not?" He cocked his head. "Mandy, don't be such a killjoy. The NYPD can work on the boring stuff, such as deciphering the social pathology of crimes and so on, because they have time to kill. On the other hand, I have no time to waste." He had the audacity to add, "I've got a couple of *Queen of the Night Brunch Matinee* tickets, and I have no intention of wasting them."

I felt like smacking him again. I couldn't believe his audacity. "Okay, so we don't need to decipher the social pathology of crimes, but we do need to figure out the whereabouts of the human-eating monster, don't we? Otherwise, we may all end up as lunch or brunch for the monster tardigrades," I pointed out.

I wasn't joking or exaggerating.

I was talking about a mass of practically imperishable and greedy creatures. Once activated, they could eat up the entire population of New York State, if not the whole world.

"Imagine it, Rick. If the monster water bears secretly proliferate in the city's underground, there will be an apocalypse," I added.

"Hmm, perhaps. That would make all those military guys deliriously happy. It'd be the first war against the immortals."

"Still, there would be lots and lots of casualties."

"Mandy, are you implying that would be *my* fault?" Rowling narrowed his eyes.

"I'm afraid so. At the very least, you'd be guilty of willful negligence." Ignoring my boss making unhappy tsk-tsk sounds, I continued. "Hey, didn't they write about how to get rid of Extremus-tardigrades?"

"The book recommends throwing them into the crater of an erupting volcano. Considering there are no such volcanoes in the vicinity, it would be more realistic to torch this place and let the whole building burn down." He flashed a wicked grin.

"Wow, that's amazingly simple," I said sarcastically. "Wait a minute. A huge candle was found burning at both scenes. Considering no one but those two boys was eaten, maybe a candle will be good enough to kill the tardigrades. Maybe they're attracted to heat, light, or something like soot."

"Then again, we want to be extra-careful. There's this bacteria called Pseudomonas radiodurans, which can live in nuclear reactor coolant, so there's no guarantee a candle can effectively kill Extremus-tardigrades. I suggest employing a military flamethrower, which would be the best option."

Rowling seemed more than thrilled about burning down this upscale condo, but I had a hunch there should be a better way to deal with this problem.

"Wait a minute," I said. "So, considering the city's not yet experiencing an apocalypse, the water bears are still being kept inactive, right?"

"I suppose so." He shrugged.

"What if we pour liquid mortar into the colony of inactivated Extremus-tardigrades? Once the mortar hardens, they can't get out of the confinement, and considering mortar isn't see-through, the creatures will stay inactive, won't they?"

Rowling crossed his arms. "Hell," he muttered. "I was looking forward to seeing this building burn."

"You know, it's not acceptable to burn down inhabited structures," I pointed out. "You wouldn't like it if your home suddenly became uninhabitable due to arson, would you?"

He cocked his head to the side. "Come on, this building's a mere show and not worth preserving, and the burning method seems much more exciting than confining the water bears in mortar."

"Okay, Rick, get creative and think of something that doesn't involve demolishing the whole building or annihilating the entire city. Ruth should be hiding a colony of monster water bears somewhere in this condo, right? I'll go find it." Leaving my purse on the coffee table, I turned on my heels.

"Wait a minute." He grabbed my arm to stop me. "You have no idea where she stored the colony, do you?"

"For starters, I'll look in the kitchen to see if she has more than one refrigerator," I said.

"Hmm, good point. When shut properly, the inside would be dark and cold." He ambled toward the dining room and into the kitchen. "Voila," he said. There was one large freezer-refrigerator and another small freezer.

"Hey, don't forget I'm the one who first suggested the fridge," I pointed out.

"Yeah, yeah." Shrugging, he opened the freezer space. "TV dinner, TV dinner, and TV dinner. Wow, this kind of dietary habit should make her antsy."

"Hey, Rick, look at this!" Peeking inside the small freezer, I let out a victorious shriek. "I think it's the colony!"

When I turned back, I was holding a rectangle-shaped Pyrex container. Instead of yummy things, such as lasagna or meatloaf, there was something resembling moss and mold.

"Are you sure?" Rowling furrowed his brow skeptically. "Let me see."

"Sure."

When I tried to hand him the container, something went terribly wrong. It slipped out of my hands and flew in the air as if it had its own will. The next thing I knew, the container crashed onto the marble floor, shattering and sprinkling the contents everywhere.

For a moment, everything stopped moving, as

if someone pushed the Stop button of the world.

"Holy crap!"

"Holy shit!"

We screamed in unison.

"What the hell have you done?" Rowling demanded while taking off his jacket.

"I-I-I…. Oh, my God, I'm so sorry!" I was shrieking in a high-pitched voice like Minnie Mouse.

"Don't panic," he said, as he switched on the gas cooker and torched his jacket. Immediately, the fire alarm started beeping, but he took out a Glock from his shoulder holster and silenced it with a bullet.

"What are *you* doing?" Now it was my turn to ask, still sounding like Minnie Mouse on meth.

"Taking care of this hot mess." He threw the burning jacket on the floor where the monster microorganisms were scattered. "Good thing this condo doesn't come with sprinklers. I knew this building's a mere show."

"Hey, I told you not to use—Eek!" I shrieked again. What used to be little spots on the kitchen floor had now grown as large as a handkerchief. In addition, the handkerchief-sized mass was vibrating and eating the suit jacket, where the fire hadn't spread yet. It seemed official that the Extremus-tardigrades had been activated.

"Shit, those motherfuckers are eating my wool clothes! Of course! That's why Ivan's and John's clothes were left behind—they were cheap synthetic material, non-organic!" Cussing, Rowling took off his shirt, trousers—everything. He kept throwing burning garments over the growing mass of little monsters. Perhaps he was trying to kill them with burning clothes, but I wasn't *really* sure if it was a good idea—his clothes might work as nutrients for the tardigrades.

I looked away from the greedy creatures and focused on my boss.

On other occasions, I might have been either shocked, startled, or aroused, for Rick Rowling was *au naturel*—except for his shoes, which he put on again after removing his pants and trunks. And, man, he had a killer bod! Bulging biceps, triceps, and pectoral muscles! And that six-pack… I really, truly felt remorseful for the world that Rick Rowling's Greek god-like body was about to vanish like smoke because of me.

Maybe it was true why everybody called me the Grim Reaper. Because of me, we were going to die. Considering Rick Rowling seemed like the only person with expertise and resources to take care of this mess, the monsters would proliferate and keep eating until there was nothing left on the surface of the Earth.

Oh, my God, I'll be responsible for the world's end! I froze at the dreaded thought. Despite the existence of fire, the colony of the monster tardigrades didn't seem to shrink at all.

"Yours looks like polyester." While I was frozen from guilt and disappointment, Rowling ripped my blouse off.

"Yes, it's polyester." I sniffed, suddenly devastated. I was totally tempted to break down and cry. The saddest part was, I was dying in cheap, crappy apparel, not something nice from Bergdorf Goodman!

"Don't even think about crying, Mandy. Extra humidity will only make them more active," he warned, giving light slaps on my cheeks. His hands moved to my back, unhooking my bra.

"Okay, I won't." I nodded. "I'm going to look for something flammable, like alcohol."

"That'll be nice." He was already throwing my blouse and bra into the flame.

I made a quick move and looked for hard liquor. Fortunately, there were bottles of rum, vodka, tequila, whiskey, and many others. I grabbed everything I could put my hands on.

Rowling took one of the tequila bottles from me, smashed the neck on the granite countertop, and poured the liquid on the burning clothes. Immediately, the flame shot up as high as six feet.

"Mandy." He turned to me.

"Yes?" Our eyes met. I noticed the orange flame flattered his intense emerald eyes and his sharp yet strong jawline. I knew it was the worst possible time, but I couldn't help thinking about how gorgeous he was.

"Take off your skirt, stockings, and panties," he said.

"Excuse me?" I gasped. I had serious regrets about having feelings for him, even for a brief moment.

"We have to burn everything, including undergarments. We don't want to risk bringing stray water bears out of the kitchen and getting eaten up by a newly proliferated colony, do we? Considering the container was literally smashed on the floor, we can't ignore the possibility of remnants on our clothes."

"Okay." I took off my skirt reluctantly, and then removed my stockings and panties. Though, considering I was already looking like someone on a losing streak during a strip poker game, taking off everything didn't seem like such a big deal. "What about our shoes?"

"We'll take them off by the threshold and toss them into the fire from outside. Let's get out of here."

Then he took my hand, and we ran toward the kitchen entrance.

When we were out of the kitchen, Rowling threw in the one remaining liquor bottle with our shoes and shut the door. I caught the muffled sounds of an explosion. I had never appreciated a kitchen door as much as that moment.

* * *

After that, things wrapped up very fast.

Using my phone, which I'd left on the coffee table in the living room, Rowling made calls: first to USCAB for backup—or rather, for sorting the mess out—and then to Detective Fender at the 34th.

Ruth MacMahon was still passed out on the sofa. I wasn't keen on admitting I was the Grim Reaper, but I was tempted to touch her, or strangle her. At this time, the only thing I liked about her was that she lived in a condo featuring full-marble floors and fireproof kitchen door. Otherwise, my new boss and I would have been burnt to a crisp, as in literally. I truly despised her.

Despite being naked, Rick Rowling was behaving as confidently as ever. I used to regard naked men sitting cross-legged on a chaise lounge as unsophisticated cavemen, but I was wrong. He was elegant, fashionable even, in spite of the situation. Every part of his body was perfectly stunning, and I wouldn't be surprised if he appeared on the front cover of Cosmopolitan magazine.

Then again, I wasn't confident at all. I didn't have a *Sports Illustrated* swimsuit edition-worthy body, and I was desperate to cover myself. Indeed, I had attempted to look for something like bath towels; however, I was restrained in Rowling's death grip, and he wouldn't let me go.

"Rick, I'd really appreciate it if you'd release my arm," I said sheepishly. I was sitting on the same chaise as him, trying my best to keep as much distance as possible between us.

"No." Putting the phone down on the table, he shook his head. "You're accident-prone. I don't want to run the risk of creating more havoc."

"I apologize for what happened. I can completely understand you're upset. After all, I jeopardized your life and everything." Trying my best not to look at him, I mumbled, "You know, I have no intention of filing a complaint, even if you fired me immediately. I'm still in my probation period, and as you know, it looks like I'm kind of the Grim Reaper, so...."

"Mandy." He pulled me close and looked me directly in the eyes. "We have a serious misunderstanding. You know what? Today was the most exciting day since I joined the Feds. It was fun."

My jaw dropped. He just said it was fun, and we were not talking about a Disney vacation. I was talking about a near-death experience, for Christ's sake!

"What's wrong with you?" I managed to ask. "Obviously, we interpret the word *fun* quite differently, don't we?"

"We're all different in our own ways," he continued, chuckling. "Okay, so at first, I was a little bit disappointed at your attempt to take safer options. Still, you made it totally hilarious. Who could have guessed you'd drop the monster water bear container on the floor and smash it?"

"That was an accident!" I protested.

"Whatever." He shrugged.

"By the way, Rick, I'm naked."

"I can see that, and I like you more when you're naked." He grinned like a cat licking cream. "Don't worry, we're not leaving here naked. Along with my clothes, yours will be delivered by the USCAB backup team."

"Speaking of backup, they could come at any time, and I can't meet them the way I'm... not dressed. Can't I at least wrap the curtain around me?" I insisted.

"Oookay. You're stubborn." He stood, ambled toward the floor-to-ceiling windows, and ripped down the curtain. "Here you are." He put the curtain on my shoulder.

"Thank you," I said, wrapping it around me. "Hey, Rick! What are you doing?" I gasped.

Starting at the other end of the curtain, he wrapped himself until our bodies were fastened a la one package.

"I'm thinking about a hundred ways you'll compensate for the brunch matinee tickets." One arm across my shoulders, he flashed his perfect set of pearly whites.

As soon as he touched my skin, I felt an electrical jolt running all over my body.

Sitting side by side, only separated by a thin silk curtain, I felt totally out of place. In an attempt to distract myself from the awkwardness, I said, "By the way, Rick, why didn't Beth provide the sample before her sister had gone too far?"

"What sample?"

"The sample you told her about," I said, pointing at the unconscious killer.

"Oh, that part? I made that up," he admitted nonchalantly. "Considering how it turned out, I was right."

I was positive his investigative method was completely against protocol, but I was already getting used to it. Call me insane, but I was even beginning to like working with him. At least it wasn't depressing.

Still, something was bugging me. "By the way, can we rule out Beth's involvement in this craziness?"

"I don't know." He shrugged. "They *are* from a family with a moderate fortune, and the sisters happen to be the only heirs. Maybe Beth was fully aware of her sister's little scheme and deliberately manipulated Ruth into taking action. Anyway, I'll think about how to make her pay, but right now, I want to focus on how you're going to pay me."

"What about this for starters?" Cupping his face in my hands, I kissed him.

"Mmm…." He kissed me back, and that time, it wasn't just a quick peck on the lips. It was a deep, hot, 'stop talkin' and just kiss me' kind of kiss.

One hand reached for my waist, the other holding one of my breasts. His lips were moving to the south.

"Hey, we can't have sex here," I stated, as he kissed my lower neck.

"I know." Between kisses, he said, "Don't forget you still owe me a lot."

And we kissed again and again and again.

When USCAB backup finally arrived and I got dressed, I realized I had to come up with a good explanation to tell my folks before I went home. A polyester skirt and blouse didn't grow into a pink Nanette Lepore dress, and my neck was covered with kiss marks.

EPILOGUE

On Monday, just two days after the near-death experience at Ruth MacMahon's condo, I was summoned to Hernandez's office.

"So, Ms. Meyer, it was not only Rick Rowling but both of you who torched 966 Park Avenue Tower, am I correct?" he asked, sporting deep worried frown lines. As he spoke, his bushy eyebrows twitched like a pair of hairy caterpillars.

"I'm afraid so," I admitted, and then added, "Fortunately, it was only the suspect's unit that got major damages. The rest of the building survived, though damaged with smoke and fire extinguisher. Good thing the kitchen was made of highly fire-resistant materials. Anyway, no one got hurt, which was great."

I tried to maintain lightheartedness in my voice. I even tried to chuckle, but in front of me, the assistant director in charge's frown lines grew deeper than the ocean. "Ms. Meyer, I was holding high expectations for you."

"I apologize for my incapability to control damage," I mumbled in apology.

I had a bad feeling about this meeting. When you're just an assistant and not a high-profile stakeholder, you don't get summoned by the head of the bureau so often, do you? I blanched, recalling the dreadful memory of spattering the deadly colony of tardigrades, instead of containing them. I was positive that Hernandez knew how I'd screwed up. As the head of New York's field office, he should have people who report to him directly about his subordinates' faux-pas and misconduct. Perhaps I was extra-antsy because I was called in just a moment before I headed to lunch. I tend to get nervous when I'm hungry. Anyway, I braced myself for the worst-case scenario, such as getting fired.

"Oh, no. You don't need to apologize." He chuckled. "Actually, you did a great job. Thanks to having the entire building evacuated, our agents were able to spot and capture a guy on Cyber's Most Wanted list. He's a big player of a racketeering enterprise and other schemes. Though this topic hasn't hit the news, the Department of State is indebted to us." When I looked at him, he was grinning ear to ear.

I didn't know the right words to say, so I smiled politely. To my astonishment, it seemed like the NYPD and DA were maintaining the case. I had no idea how and where they would put the monster tardigrades in the trial, but Hernandez didn't seem to care about the issue.

"Now that we've saved them the trouble of rewarding three million dollars to some civilian whoever might or might not have helped us find the guy. They owe us big time. Great job, Ms. Meyer."

At first, I didn't know how to react to this news, but it soon dawned on me that three million dollars was a lot of money. I would be very happy if I saved three million. Not that I had such money. To tell the truth, I would be deliriously happy if I could offset my 300K of student loan.

"Isn't that great?" I said casually, "Sir, may I ask for 10 percent of that money as a bonus?"

"Hahaha! That's funny." He laughed drily, but

his eyes were not smiling. "Was that intended to be the joke of the year? Or are you seriously asking for a bonus after jeopardizing the entire city of annihilation?"

"Well, I was just saying."

Just like the first day, he wished me good luck and I was released.

When I came out of his office, Rick Rowling was standing outside the door. "Hey. That took long."

I shrugged. "He was deliriously happy. I still have my job." Then I let out a sigh of relief.

"Oh, yeah?" One corner of his lips quirked into a smile. "Let's go for lunch. I'm famished."

* * *

After eating at a nice Italian place in Tribeca, we were taking a stroll through Pier 26.

It was one of the most beautiful autumn days in the city. Sunny, warm and nice, with a cool breeze coming off the Hudson River. People were walking, jogging, and kayaking. Everyone seemed happy in their own way—except one.

He was dressed in a revealing outfit of neon green and hot pink, like a female dancer at Brazilian samba carnivals. With his big hair, boa headdress and high heels, his outfit screamed 'FESTIVE'—literally, as he wore a huge necklace that spelled the exact word. Still, 'festive' was the least appropriate word to describe his mood. He was crying with his hair messed up, mascara running down his face, and a huge laceration on the side out of his abdomen.

"Oh, my God…." I instinctively clutched Rowling's arm.

"What? Don't tell me you're finally aroused enough to get it on with me. First of all, having sex in front of spectators at a public place is a big no-no. Secondly, you should have slept with me on Saturday when you had a chance to—"

"Rick, it's not a time to be a smartass!" I hissed. "Can't you see there's an assault victim in front of us?"

"What are you talking about? Where's the victim?" He furrowed his brow.

"Come on! Can't you see the drag queen over there? Just because you're a New Yorker doesn't entitle you to be totally indifferent to someone suffering! He's about five-foot-ten, wearing a samba dancer costume with a 'FESTIVE' necklace around his neck. And he's…." As I explained, I realized no one else seemed to have noticed the victim.

"Mandy, are you sure you're not joking?" When Rowling stopped, my eyes met with those of the drag queen's. Before I had a chance to avert my gaze, he was in front of my face. Instead of walking, he floated toward me.

"Hey, sweetheart. You can see me, right?" he demanded, reaching me with outstretched arms. When he came near me, I saw blood still oozing from the wound in his belly. And something that looked like his colon was peekabooing from the wound.

"Eeeeek!" I shrieked. So I went to medical school, but I was never good at dealing with bodily fluid. In addition, it didn't help that his hands passed through my body when he tried to grab my shoulders. "He's bleeding! He's drifting, and he's bleeding!"

"Actually, he doesn't exist, at least the way

we can recognize him." Rowling shook his head, the drag queen purring at him.

"Ooh… he's sooo hot, isn't he?" The drag queen winked at me.

"Oh, my god, he just winked at me! Rick, am I hallucinating?" I slapped my forehead. "Did I go insane?"

By that time, people were glancing at me from the distance, as if I were some sort of crazy. Okay, maybe they thought I was a head case, but at least they weren't indifferent to me.

"Oh, my God! I knew you could see me! You also know what I'm talking about, right? Finally, I found someone who can communicate with me! I'm soooo delighted!" Now it was the drag queen's turn to shriek.

I opened my mouth, my jaw dropping.

I was shocked, dazed, and totally overwhelmed. I might not be the sharpest knife in the kitchen, but there was one thing I was sure of: I was not only seeing but talking to the ghost of a murdered drag queen.

I grabbed Rowling's arm in a death-grip. "Rick, now he's saying that he's super-happy to finally find someone who can see and communicate with him."

"I see. Mandy, ask him if he's Jackson Frederick Orchard, the actor who was stabbed to death on his way back home from a Gay Pride event in June," Rowling ordered.

"Yes, yes, yeees!" The drag queen answered enthusiastically. Floating and bouncing, he continued. "It's me! I was totally stabbed by this SOB on my way home that night. Can you believe it? How unacceptable! What a loser to stab such a lovely, defenseless girl! I had just landed this big role in Aladdin, and I was going to be the next shining star! They haven't caught the guy, and I totally, definitely insist that someone must catch him." He rambled on and on. "By the way, call me Jackie."

"Okay, Jackie…," I mumbled.

"Jackie who?" Rowling nudged me.

"He admitted being Jackson Frederick Orchard, and he prefers to be called Jackie," I explained.

"I prefer to be referred to as *she*, not *he*." Jackie made a tsk-tsk sound.

"Ooookay. Jackie prefers to be treated as a lady." I fought an urge to roll my eyes until they popped out of their sockets.

Rowling's eyebrows went north. "I didn't know you could talk to dead people. Hey, with your skill, we can solve more and more cases with much ease, and we can interview murder victims to dig up even more. Why didn't you tell me earlier?"

"Because I've never communicated with a dead person before." I sighed, having a seriously hard time keeping up with my new ability.

Last month, people started dying moments after my touch, and now I'm communicating with a dead person. Maybe next month, I'll be able to summon Martians.

I didn't know where my life was heading and, to be honest, I didn't want to know.

Jackie, on the other hand, was hovering around Rowling, showering my boss with kisses.

Rowling shuddered visibly. "Why do I feel cold and eerie?"

"Perhaps that has something to do with Jackie the ghost drag queen kissing all over you," I pointed out.

"What?" Rowling swung his hands as if attempting to whack pestering bugs. "Hey, Jackie, don't ever try to molest me! I know a hotshot exorcist, and I can always cast you out of this world. Did you hear that?" he threatened, pointing at an empty space in the air.

"Yeah, yeah. I'm scared." Jackie shrugged. "Exorcists are like psychics, right? They're so overrated. I tried to communicate with so-called psychics, but none of them could even see me, much less talk with me. A bunch of shmucks."

I made a sympathetic noise. Then I turned to Rowling. "Rick, Jackie's upset that none of those so-called psychics were able to communicate with her."

"I see. 99.9 percent of them are frauds." Rowling nodded. "Where's Jackie?"

"She's here." I gestured to the floating drag queen.

Rowling turned in that direction. "Hi, Jackie. I'm Rick Rowling, head of Paranormal Cases Division at the FBI. This is Mandy, my assistant. I need to ask you some questions to catch your killer."

"Go ahead, Rick. Let's bust this bastard!" Jackie pumped his... um, *her* fists. Then she turned to me. "Mandy, sugar, will you be an angel and help me communicate with Rick?" She winked.

"Um...okay," I agreed, but I couldn't help recoiling, mostly because I couldn't tear my eyes off the ghost's exposed intestines.

Jackie pouted. "Excuse me, Mandy? I see you cringe every time I talk to you. Why? Do you think I'm some kind of a monster? Are you discriminating against me because I'm... different?"

"Um... I'm so sorry," I apologized. "I didn't

mean to treat you badly. It's just… you know, I'm not accustomed to talking to someone with her guts sticking out of the body."

"Oopsie." Jackie glanced at her wound and shrugged. Stretching the pink Spandex dress to cover up, she asked, "Now, better?"

"I guess." I rolled my eyes. *Who could have guessed Spandex was so stretchy?*

Strangely, as we talked, the ghost of a drag queen looked slightly more realistic.

Thus began my new and wicked career........

About the author

Hi! My name is Lotta Smith. I'm the author of Paranormal in Manhattan Mysteries and Kelly Kinki Mysteries. I love everything comedy, from novels, TVs, to movies. In my teenage days, I was addicted to mysteries that involves amateur sleuth duo of a hot male professor and a quirky female student—with a light touch of romance sprinkled on top. So I went to medical school, partly because I wanted to see *real* dead bodies, and mostly because I was determined to meet sexy professors (specializing forensic pathology, perhaps) and go a-sleuthin'.

I got to see dead bodies and learn about the danger of petting zoos (sometimes, kids have their lips bitten off by…say, a pony!) but unfortunately, sexy professors were absolutely nonexistent. Recently, I realized that I'm a hopeless *un*romantic.

I'm hard at work writing new books.

Books by Lotta Smith

PI Assistant Extraordinaire Mysteries:
Book 1: Ghostly Murder: http://amzn.to/2O4aWJ4

> *A murder in a locked room…*
> *A faceless ghost…*
> *Throw in a cross-dressing detective-savant*
> *plus his assistant extraordinaire in this new mystery*
> *series!*

A high profile murder calls for a high profile detective.

When the famous Sushi Czar is found dead in a room that's locked from the inside, the evidence just doesn't add up. Of course a killer ghost (supernatural killer) is no match for the deductive skills of Michael Archangel. The fabulous cross-dressing former FBI agent can rock a set of sky high stilettos and assemble clues like puzzle pieces, but can he actually prove a ghost committed murder?

Only his assistant knows for sure. Former housewife and London socialite Kelly Kinki (it's Kinki ending with an I not a Y) may someday be the Watson to Archangel's Holmes, but for now, she's following orders, coveting his fashion sense and learning from the master PI that there's something truly fishy about this case.

CHAPTER 1

There's a first time for everything.

I was walking in the forest all by myself. It was a sunny day in late March, but in the shadows of tall trees, it was dark, cold, and creepy. Also, having a group of crows—a.k.a. a *murder* of crows—squawking over my head did nothing to calm my nerves.

Don't get me wrong. I was not an adventurer wannabe or a plant hunter wandering about some exotic forest in the middle of nowhere with a totally unpronounceable name, such as *Tweebuffelsmeteenskootmorsdoodgeskietfontein* in Africa. On the contrary, I was one of those so-called city workers. My job title was the personal assistant to a certain private investigator based in McLean, Virginia.

I was in Arlington, the 'good' suburb of Washington DC. Though there was a metro station in walking distance, this part of the town was very quiet, giving it the feel of a godforsaken land. I wasn't exaggerating. Maybe the fact that a man's dead body was found nearby had something to do with my perception. In addition, considering he was stabbed to death, this neighborhood might not be such a good area. Oh, did I mention there was some wacko serial rapist still running loose in the neighborhood? As a woman with no expertise in martial arts, I had a gazillion reasons to be spooked.

Walking in the forest wasn't something I was doing by choice. Michael Archangel, my eccentric employer with a diva personality, made me do so. My mission was to look for either pantyhose, a ski mask, or big granny panties. Any of those items were supposed to help my employer with his most recent case, but I couldn't figure out why or how. Anyway, I had never dreamed about going treasure-hunting for potentially used undergarments in the urban forest at the age of twenty-nine.

When I was a kid, I wanted to be an alchemist or a doctor. But the reality wasn't rosy enough to realize either of my childhood dreams. First of all, there was no alchemist school. In addition, my test score wasn't good enough for premed programs. So my mom and fifth—or was it sixth?—faux-dad sent me to a finishing school in Switzerland where I mastered the art of eating an orange using a knife and a fork. After that, I became a housewife in London, obtained a bachelor's degree in art, and then I got a divorce. People in Europe, especially rich people in London, still called me 'the bitch who used to be married to that swindler' a.k.a. the man who had committed the largest investment scam in the history of Great Britain.

Here's my point: Education is so overrated.

My name is Kelly Kinki. Yes, it's my real name as written on my birth certificate. No, my surname is not a joke. And no, I'm not into kinky sex. Kinky or otherwise, it had been a while since I had sex.

As I thought about sex, I realized how much I hated walking through the creepy woods. I could think of much better things to do—such as tackling crossword puzzles or building a robot vacuum cleaner from scratch—but sometimes, you had to do what you had to do.

All of the sudden, one of the crows let out an especially menacing squawk as something started chirping and vibrating at the same time, startling me.

"Holy crap!"

A second later, I realized it was coming from my purse and reached for my phone.

"Hello? What can I do for you, Mr. Archangel?" I said to the person on the other end, who happened to be the one responsible for my current situation.

There was no response.

"Hello? Mr. Archangel?"

Still nothing.

From the other end, I could hear muffled voices. I recalled a bunch of retired gentlemen, who resided in the neighborhood, gathering at the crime scene. When I left there, they were busy gossiping. In my mind's eyes, I could almost see and hear them cracking jokes and laughing their *as*—I mean, laughing their *pants* off. A moment later, I finally got a whispered response from Archangel.

"Password."

"What? Password? What are you talking about?" I said, puzzled.

"You need to provide the password of Michael Archangel Investigations."

"Excuse me? I've got your name on my caller ID. And it's my voice. You can recognize me from my voice, can't you?"

"No. You sound different," he said. "Actually, you sound pretty much annoyed."

"Come on, so I'm pretty much annoyed right now, but still, it's me. Besides that, you're the one who's calling my phone, so you should know—" I was tempted to go on with my rant, but I realized it was easier to just tell the password.

"All right! I'll tell the password." Then I stopped short. What was the password? I knitted my eyebrows. It was something about artists. Oh yeah—Matisse, Bonnard, and Rothko—that was it.

"Matisse, Bonnard," I said my part and waited for him to say "Rothko" but—

"Okay, let's get to the point."

"Hey!" I protested. "You're supposed to finish the password before getting to the point. I said 'Matisse, Bonnard' and you're supposed to say 'Rothko.' Without your finishing, the password isn't complete!"

"What are you babbling, Kelly? It's me, Michael Archangel. You should be able to recognize me from my voice. Otherwise, you must be affected with an early-onset of Alzheimer's."

All right, he had a point. The password was pretty much worthless since I knew I was talking to Archangel. His voice was deep, husky, and somewhat seductive, per usual. In addition, I knew no one else as fuc—I mean, *freaking* annoying as him.

"So, what's up, Mr. Archangel? Any progress?"

"Yeah. The cops found the item I was looking for. I knew it was somewhere in the ground. Anyway, you can come back to the tennis court."

"What? So you sent me to this creepy forest fully knowing I wouldn't be the one to find the granny panties?"

"Actually, the discovered item turned out to be a ghost mask."

"That's not the point. You sent me, of all people, to go into this deep, spooky, and potentially dangerous forest for a wild goose chase of a ghost mask you didn't even bother to mention in the first place. On top of it all, I'm talking about these woods located near the site where a twenty-four-year-old female office worker was nearly raped last night for Pete's sake!" I spat.

I knew about her because, this morning, local news was all about this serial rapist in Arlington. In the past month, at least five women had been brutally raped. I was more than concerned about my own safety.

"Good thing you're much older than twenty-four years old," was Archangel's reply.

"Excuse me? That's not the point." I continued. "This rapist has not yet been ID'd, much less arrested. Has it ever come to your mind that the rapist is still hiding in the darkness of these woods, determined to assault another young, innocent, and defenseless woman, such as your assistant? Imagine it. I might become his next prey. Aren't you worried about me?"

Without responding to my bullets of questions, he said, "Come back to the tennis court pronto. If you don't come back before I finish wrapping up the case, I'll leave without you."

And the line went dead.

Words like *manners* and *protocol* must be missing from my employer's dictionary.

Man, I really, *really* hated this job.

Book 2: Immortal Eyes: http://amzn.to/1T4DKC3

> *Serial murder with a sick ritual...*
> *The most unusual way to use Eggs Benedict...*
> *The mismatched duo's race against time...*

Former London socialite Kelly Kinki doesn't always see eye to eye with her sexy-as-hell boss Michael Archangel, but she'll follow the brilliant, cross-dressing detective anywhere to help solve their latest case.

Kelly was happy to lay her rep as the Dragon Lady to rest when she moved across the pond, but to catch an eyeball snatching serial killer she'll have to put her skills at fire breathing to the test once again.

A gruesome autopsy, a visit with her ex, and a shocking encounter with a killer compete for craziest day on the job, but nothing can hold a candle to a glimpse of her boss in the buff.

Can Kelly and Archangel solve the case? The ayes have it. PI's that is.

* * *

Chapter 1

There's a first time for everything.

I was at a medical examiner's office in rural Virginia. It was my first visit to this place and, actually, it also happened to be my very first trip to a morgue. I was there to attend the autopsy of a woman who allegedly had fallen victim to a brutal murder. So far, I'd seen more than my share of corpses in the past four months; however, I usually saw them at crime scenes and not morgues.

I didn't know much about the statistics of murders, but I had seen lots of homicide victims since starting this job. In the beginning, I kept track of the body count, but I stopped counting after hitting ten on the third day of my current employment. Later, I learned it was just a temporary thing—one of those crazy, busy times— the "on-season" of killing. Anyway, who knew murders had on-seasons? And I'm not talking about Walmart jobs during the holiday season or the wedding industry in June.

My name is Kelly Kinki. Yes, it's my real name as written on my birth certificate. No, I'm not into kinky sex, and no, I'm not making this surname thing up. I'm twenty-nine years old, half Italian-English American and half Japanese. Currently, I'm divorced with no intention or anticipation of a new romantic relationship, much less marriage.

Been there, done that. No thank you very much.

Right then, my mind was completely centered on my career. And guess what, thinking about myself as a super-cool, classy, and oh-so-savvy sleuth—the assistant extraordinaire, to be precise—totally made me happy. The hard bench chair I sat on was no Cassina, and with the faded grayish-green color scheme, sad taste in décor—or lack thereof—and chilly yet stale air, the morgue's waiting room was depressing at the best of times. But I was optimistic. In fact, I was feeling kind of flamboyant because I really, *really* liked the idea of visiting the morgue in line of my job. First of all, I loved the *CSI* TV series, and the prospect of seeing a live autopsy was totally thrilling. Besides that, it was not like the morgues were open to the public so that anybody could take a sightseeing tour and attend an autopsy, right? Having access to this facility was a real privilege.

In my mind, I was picturing myself as a female version of Dr. John Watson, only less geeky. Maybe by taking a part in the autopsy, I might come up with something that could lead to a breakthrough—just like super-assistants of brilliant detectives in fictions do all the time. Maybe I could even kick some ass like a badass assistant, too. In my opinion, it was often the assistant extraordinaire who should get the credit for disentangling the mystery before his/her boss did.

Something warm and fuzzy started to bubble up in my stomach. It wasn't the aftereffect of a lunch burrito. I had to use a great amount of self-restraint to keep myself from singing, *"For the first time in forever, I'll be watching an autopsy!"* like a certain Princess of Arendelle.

I didn't realize I was smiling until I heard, "Why don't you stop grinning like an idiot?" in a deep, husky voice, which belonged to Michael Archangel, the private investigator I worked for, who was sitting next to me on the same bench.

How I managed to forget his presence, I didn't know. If nothing else, the delicate yet distinct scent of Higher Energy by Dior, his fragrance de jour, should have alerted me to his presence.

No thanks to his voice, I was snapped back to the reality that it was him who had access to the morgue, not me. I hadn't clarified with the morgue, but considering I had no authority or qualification, they wouldn't have granted me permission to attend the autopsy if I went there all by myself. I also realized a *real* badass woman wouldn't imagine singing like a Disney Princess while sitting in the morgue's waiting room. The truth was, I wasn't very sure if I *wanted* to attend the autopsy at all.

I was no Dr. Watson. I had no background in medicine. The closest experience I'd ever had with this particular field was having a pediatrician and an orthopedic surgeon as ex-faux-dads. It was the first time for me to see a cadaver getting cut open. The corpses I had seen often had a hole or two, but I had never seen the human innards peekabooing from inside of the body cavity, saying something like "Yoo-hoo?"

As I anticipated this new experience, a gazillion butterflies went wild in my stomach. Okay, so the earlier flamboyance and faux-hardboiled tone were only parts of my façade to hide my nervousness. And speaking of body contents, I wasn't sure if I'd be able to keep my lunch burrito where it belonged.

Discreetly, I took a deep breath to calm my nerves and regain my composure. "I didn't realize you were watching every step of mine, but thanks for your keen attention anyway. I'm flattered," I said nonchalantly.

"Ha." With a snort, Archangel's candy-apple-colored lips curled into a sarcastic smirk. "Don't get me wrong; it's hard to miss someone sitting by my side babbling silly things with goofy grin pasted on her face, especially when this special someone starts drooling."

I felt around my lips with my fingertips, only to find the area completely drool-free.

"I wasn't drooling. You tricked me!" I narrowed my eyes.

"It's because you're such a good comic relief to poke fun at, Kelly," he had the audacity to admit.

"But look on the bright side. It was just a joke and not a con. Hey, speaking of a con, did I mention I in no compare to the lying, cheating, jilting, swindling, oh-so-disturbing excuse for a human douchebag who happens to be your ex-husband?" With a lighthearted chuckle, he added, "No pun intended."

Biting my lip, I toyed with the idea of kicking him really hard in the shin. This cra…I mean, *nonsense*, of him dissing Warren and my past marriage was just getting old, and it was oh-so-tempting to finally make a point. But I thought better of it. First off, kicking your employer runs a potentially hazardous risk for your job security. Secondly, most of his words were accurate, especially the part about my ex being a con—as in being a convicted conman. I didn't want to reinforce his cocksureness by getting upset. That would only tip him off that yours truly, indeed, had *feelings* for my ex-husband.

So instead of kicking him, I retorted, "I never drool!"

"Hey, Kelly." Flashing the perfect set of pearly whites, Archangel nudged my elbow. "Look what you've done to her." I followed his gaze and spotted the female receptionist. She was practically gaping at us from behind the counter. My eyes met with hers. I tried a polite, social smile that implied I was not her enemy. She averted her gaze.

"See?" He cocked his head. "You've managed to creep her out in five minutes. What a shame. Now I'm labeled as a PI who's stuck with a weird assistant from La-La Land. Come on, I've got a reputation to maintain." As he shook his head, shining locks of his long, auburn hair swayed like dancing waves.

"I see, so you've got a reputation to maintain." Rephrasing his words, I gave him an up-and-down look. His attire consisted of a skintight, above-the-knee-length dress in vivid magenta and purple fishnet stockings paired with fuck-me-if-you-can high heels. Okay, so the colorful attire flattered his alabaster complexion and the totally gorgeous hair that went midway down his back. Even the heavy makeup wasn't laughable.

Yes, you heard me right. I said he was dressed like a woman. I'm not making any of this up. His outfit de jour was described as skimpy and eye-catching, at best. It was not his Halloween costume on an account that it was early April, not the last day of October. Did I mention that cross-dressing was his "casual/business" attire? I didn't know and didn't want to know what he wore for black-tie events.

I glanced back at the receptionist, who was shaking her head as if trying to clear away the many thoughts running through her mind. I suspected she was taken aback—no, that would be an understatement. I wouldn't be surprised if her brain was caught in a temporary cerebral arrest. Archangel had that effect for many people. Basically, unlike L.A. or Miami, seeing a transvestite in rural Virginia was a very rare occasion, which alone counted as an element of surprise. There was another major element called confusion. Indeed, to the casual eye, his appearance was very confusing. I'm not talking about an esthetically challenged dude playing dress up as a geisha.

He wasn't ugly—lucky him—thanks to inheriting high cheekbones, baby-blue eyes, a well-sculpted nose in a perfect shape that would make Cleopatra cry with envy, and a tall, slender figure from both his mother—Miss California—and grandmother—Miss Greek—he managed to appear almost as strikingly gorgeous as a woman. At least in photos.

Speaking of photos, I supposed perhaps she had seen the pictures of him in the morning paper. Newspapers often carried his photographs. As a Virginia-based PI, he usually consulted with law enforcement, such as the FBI, and worked on tricky, weird, or even the most impossible cases. As a matter of fact, he happened to be a good detective—not just good, but top-notch. He always cracked difficult cases quickly, and as result, newspapers, magazine articles, websites, and sometimes even TV shows reported his accomplishments.

Then again, seeing him in person was a whole different story. Archangel happened to have an even bigger impact in person. He still looked *almost* like a woman. To be precise, he looked more like a supermodel than a woman. I mean, it's not like supermodels look like the rest of us *real* women, right? Those tall, skinny girls are byproducts of women-hating men who dominate the fashion industry and set out to punish us real women by force-feeding us distorted body images, just because we have curves and boobs.

Okay, enough with my little speech. I had mixed feelings about my employer's looks. I know his outfit preference was none of my business, and I believe everyone's entitled to express themselves through fashion. I also appreciated he was the one who caught all the attention, not me. I was the shadow. I enjoyed my invisibility. Then again, it got *a little* awkward when total strangers would stare at us, chattering about 'That totally dazzling supermodel,' and they went on like, 'Who's she? The little one standing next to her? An assistant wannabe? Doesn't she look so mediocre and a little bit heavy?'

And it got *a little* annoying when Archangel caught such chatter and would announce, 'Did you hear that? They think I'm pretty and you're not!'

Did I mention he has a diva personality?

Yeah, it's pretty clear, I ain't no size two. But in my defense, I've got the boobs, uterus, ovaries, and everything a girl needs. Besides that, it's totally rude to judge people based on the physical features for Pete's sake! I might be described as a petite woman, but that doesn't make me *the little one*. I'm the assistant, not a wannabe. Besides that, if you looked carefully, Archangel's jaw was a little bit too strong for a woman and he has an Adam's apple. At 6'3" with lots of toned muscles, what he resembled the most was a Greek Goddess with excessive growth hormone. Or Poseidon in drag.

"Mr. Archangel, why do you think I'm the one who's responsible for spooking her out? Has it ever occurred to you that maybe you're the one who's grabbing her full attention?" I asked.

"Why?" Without answering my question, he arched an eyebrow.

"First of all, she's looking in our direction in general, so both of us are in her sights, and..." I struggled with the words.

"And?" he probed, tapping the backrest of the bench chair with his fingers, which sported nail polish in the same shade of color as the lips.

I was ready to tell him, "And... with all due respect, a giant transvestite is very eye-catching—or rather, an eyesore?" Then it dawned on me that maybe dissing your employer might not be a good move. Call me desperate, but I wasn't made of money and I needed to pay my credit card balance. Unlike Mom, I wasn't a rich-husband-magnet, which meant I really needed to keep my job as a personal assistant to this huge, cross-dressing, brilliant-yet-cynical detective. Maybe I shouldn't have purchased those pricy pillows from Neiman Marcus, but they were so worth it. You want to invest in high-quality pillows to ensure beauty sleep and sweet dreams, especially when you see murdered corpses on a regular basis.

Also, I knew the chances of my scoring other gainful employment anytime soon were practically nonexistent. My resume wasn't something described as highly-decorated. On top of all that, it's not like having lost my last employer in a tragic murder— which wasn't my fault but made me look like a jinx— *and* being an ex-wife of a notorious swindler would catch a potential employer's attention in a good way, would it?

Yes, I was desperate. So much for an independent woman ready to kick ass.

"Kelly? Tell me why you think I'm the one who's creeping her out." Crossing his long legs, Archangel pressed on.

"Well…" With all due respect, I furrowed my eyebrows like a confused third-grader struggling to grasp the concept of division. "What was I thinking? Isn't it odd that I can't recollect whatever was in my head?"

"Ha. You need to get a head CT to see if you've got a brain at all." Archangel gave a throaty, husky, oh-so-manly laugh. Did I mention his voice was often a dead giveaway for his otherwise confusing gender? When I first met him, I thought he must be gay, but I wasn't so sure any more. I knew his sexual orientation was none of my business, and I respected people with every sexuality, but for a guy who opted to wear women's clothes, Archangel was pretty much lacking delicacy.

Turning my face away from him, I stuck out my tongue. Very mature, I knew. So far, my job duties were one part secretary, one part chauffeur, and one part personal chef. Not to mention being a part-time comic, or rather, laughing stock. Unlike brilliant detectives in literature, Archangel didn't need much assisting when it came to investigation and solving cases. Just like fictional detectives, he was crazy and tended to torment his precious little assistant, having a chuckle at my expense.

I was an assistant extraordinaire who outshone the detective only in my fantasy, and in reality, I was merely a newbie assistant and a butt of jokes to this huge, cross-dressing detective.

It really sucked when the gap between your fancy daydream and the hard, cold, stone-hearted reality was so huge.

Book 3: Deadly Vision: http://amzn.to/1og0Pp9

A sweet n' cold murder…
A newbie, pathetic agent…
And a hot mess…

PI Assistant extraordinaire Kelly Kinki is back, and she's stuck between a hunk and a hard case.

A popular college student has been murdered after visiting a local ice cream shop. The suspect list is short and sweet, but with a fledgling FBI agent tagging along on their investigation, Kelly and her drop dead gorgeous boss Michael Archangel have an extra scoop of trouble.

Trading his dress for a suit and hitting DC's top ten list of eligible bachelors may be business as usual for Archangel, but with a hopeless newbie screwing up the case and Kelly revving up his libido, solving this seemingly ordinary murder might not be cake for America's answer to Sherlock Holmes.

* * *

CHAPTER 1

There's a first time for everything.

I was engaged in a tight lip-lock with Michael Archangel, a Virginia-based private investigator and my employer.

There should have been a sequence of events that led to the incident, but I couldn't recall anything at all. And for full disclosure, I was way too preoccupied with the current action to care about how I ended up in a hot kiss with him.

Just like in cartoons, the angel part of me was sitting on my right shoulder, screaming things like "Hello! What's happened to your professionalism? Don't you have anything like work ethics?" And the devil part of me was hooting, jumping, and cheering me from on my other shoulder. "Go, Kelly, go! Think about it, you're not getting any younger!" She was a really naughty devil.

As a professional woman with work ethics and dignity, I didn't listen to the devil and started listening to the angel, and…no, that's a lie. I didn't listen to the angel. Call me an unethical slut, but I was falling for the devil's words.

For a brief moment, our lips parted. I opened my eyes. His baby blues were staring at me so intensely, they seemed a shade or two darker than usual.

He cupped my face in his hands.

"Are you ready?" he whispered. His voice sounded oh-so-sweet on my ears. Then he brushed away my hair and planted a light peck on my forehead.

I mumbled something that meant nothing and everything. Then I realized he was shirtless and I was only one slutty Agent Provocateur bra and a thong away from…*gulp!* the bedroom.

Breathing hard and admiring his Greek god-like physique, I struggled with his belt buckle, which didn't unbuckle easily. I shivered as Archangel unhooked my bra with just a snap of his fingers.

I closed my eyes. He was reaching south, and then…

Did You Like *Wicked for Hire*?

Let everyone know by posting a review on Amazon.

When you finish this book, you can access Amazon **http://amzn.to/1ZV76mZ** and rate this book. You can also post your thoughts on Facebook and Twitter. How cool is that? Be the first one of your friends to use this innovative technology. Your friends get to know what you're reading and I, for one, will be forever grateful to you.

Happy reading!

XOXO, Lotta Smith

Made in the USA
Lexington, KY
12 July 2018